SECOND FIDDLE

SECOND FIDDLE

· ·

A Sizzle & Splat Mystery

Ronald Kidd

Troll Associates

A TROLL BOOK, published by Troll Associates,
Mahwah, NJ 07430

Copyright © 1988 by Ronald Kidd

Published by arrangement with E.P. Dutton, a division of
NAL Penguin Inc. For information address E.P. Dutton, a division
of NAL Penguin Inc., 2 Park Avenue, New York, New York 10016.

First Troll Printing, 1990

Printed in the United States of America.

10 9 8 7 6 5 4 3 2 1

ISBN 0-8167-1823-7

to Carol and Bill Loscutoff
and their three-piece orchestra—
Paul, Lilli, and Susie

I

● ● ● ● ● ● ●

I guess it all started the day Freddy Fosselman heard the bass drum talk.

It was spring vacation, and the Pirelli Youth Orchestra had scheduled daily practice sessions to read through some new music. I was sitting in the trumpet section, warming up for Monday's rehearsal, idly wondering who was the first guy to stick brass tubing in his mouth and blow on it, when Freddy came hurrying across the room, his eyes the size of tambourines.

"Sizzle, come quick," he bleated, "it's the bass drum!"

I glanced over at the percussion section and nodded. "Sure is, Fred. Big as life." With Freddy, it was always best to stay calm. He tended to get a little hysterical, like the time he mistook a pair of cymbals for a fleet of Martian landing craft.

"No, I mean . . ." He looked around, then leaned close and said in a low voice, "It's talking to me."

"What's it saying?"

"Something about a labor dispute," he said. "It's threatening to go on strike."

"A drum go on strike? Bad pun, Fred."

"I'm not kidding. Come see for yourself."

I set down my trumpet and followed him. We made a strange pair, Freddy and I—a shrimpy junior high school drummer and a five-foot-eleven female trumpet player who'd seen the better side of seventeen. Odd as it was, though, it's the kind of thing you run across in that curious blend of stuffed shirt and T-shirt known as the youth orchestra.

On the way across the rehearsal hall we passed the tuba preserve, inhabited by that very rarest of species, the Arthur Hadley Reavis Pauling III, common name Splat. This creature, not to be confused with Homo sapiens, is known for its greasy hair, bad complexion, scrawny limbs, and sunken chest. Often sighted near record stores and concert halls, the Splat can be identified by its duck-footed walk and distinctive high-pitched cackle.

Today the beast was sprawled across three chairs, eyes closed, mouth open, wheezing like a cheap accordion.

"Yo, Sleeping Beauty," I said as we walked by.

Splat stirred, emitting something halfway between a yawn and a belch. He was wearing a shirt bearing the words *Honk if you love Humperdinck.*

"When the proprietor returns," I said, "could you tell him to meet us in the percussion section?"

Approaching the bass drum with Freddy, I didn't see or hear anything unusual. The snare drum, timpani, and xylophone sat nearby, as always. Since the hour was still early, there was no one in the vicinity except us.

"Freddy," I said, "have you been watching 'Twilight Zone' reruns again?"

Then I heard it. "Fosselman is unfair! Fosselman is unfair!" The voice was male and tinny. It was coming from the bass drum.

"See?" said Freddy, his eyebrows dancing nervously.

I checked the area for pixies, leprechauns, and elves, with no success.

"As spokesdrum for the Brotherhood of Associated Noisemakers and Gongs (BANG)," the voice went on, "I hereby make the following demands. Item one: Effective immediately, all drum beatings shall cease. Interaction with union members will be limited to taps, pats, and caresses."

I glanced at Freddy. "Caresses?"

"Item two: No sticks, with the exception of peppermint and licorice, will be permitted within twenty feet of the percussion section. Item three: Between rehearsals, union members will no longer be locked in a closet. Instead, living space will be provided, with convenient access to shopping and recreational facilities."

As the voice continued its demands, I noticed a wire leading down the drum stand and along the floor. "Stay here, Fred," I said. "I'll be back in a minute."

I followed the wire through the string section and

around to the far side of the rehearsal hall, where it went under a door leading to an adjoining room. Very quietly I pushed the door open a crack and peered in.

– Lounging on the floor, his back propped against the wall, was Myron "My" Mann, principal French hornist and resident practical joker of the Pirelli Youth Orchestra. He was speaking into a small hand-held microphone. "Item six: Choice of percussion instruments shall no longer be left to the whim of the composer. From this point forward, the appropriate instrument will be determined by a majority vote of union members."

I swung open the door and walked in. "Dictating material for your memoirs, Myron?"

Before he could respond, I took the microphone and spoke into it. "This is Prudence Szyznowski. As Myron's close personal friend, I feel the time has come to bring his problem out into the open. The truth, ladies and gentlemen, is that Myron Mann has a serious problem with women's underwear."

Myron blanched. "I'll take that microphone!" he croaked, snatching the offending implement from my hand.

I shrugged. "Sorry, My, but somebody had to say it." I walked back into the rehearsal hall, where a group had gathered around Freddy and the bass drum. It included Splat, fully revived by now, and Vidor Pirelli, founder and director of the orchestra.

Splat nodded to me as I approached. "Courageous statement," he said. "Very gutsy stuff."

Freddy looked from me to the bass drum and back again. "Will somebody please tell me what's going on?"

"It seem," explained Pirelli, his speech an exotic brew

4

of unidentifiable accents and inflections, "that Mr. Myron Mann have been pulling our feet once again."

Just then, the Mann himself slunk back into the room, eyes averted, trying to blend into the scenery.

"Hey, Myron," called Splat, " 'Sixty Minutes' is on the phone. Something about a charge account at Lulu's Lace Emporium."

Pirelli touched Splat's shoulder. "Now, now, Arthur, we mustn't be too hard on our Myron. Besides," he said, a twinkle in his eye, "I myself may have some little surprise for him."

"What kind of surprise?" I asked.

"The best kind of all," he replied. "A musical surprise."

Thirty minutes later Pirelli was at the podium, Myron was seated next to me in the brass section, and everything was back to normal—or as normal as things get in an orchestra where the three B's aren't Bach, Beethoven, and Brahms, but bicycles, braces, and bubble gum.

"My dear young friends," said Pirelli, "you are certainly welcome to our special rehearsals of springing break. For most of the year we clean and polish some very few pieces to play before a crowd. But this week we are having the privilege to try many new musics simply for ourself." He beamed, the way your grandfather might smile after pressing a shiny silver dollar into your hand.

"But before we begin to start," Pirelli went on, "I have a great pleasure of announcement. As you know, our concertmaster Anthony Formica have just left us, so this past month we hold auditions to take his place. Today I am most happy to introduce our brand-new concertmaster. Please to take your first bow, Mr. Kevin Lim!"

A young man rose from his chair at the front of the violin section. He was perhaps sixteen years old, slight of build, and wore neatly pressed slacks and a knit shirt. Smiling shyly, he nodded his head, then quickly sat down.

"If Kevin's name of Lim sound familiar to some of you," said Pirelli, "this is because his father is the proud and famous Mr. Bradford Lim, concertmaster of our very own Los Angeles Philharmonic Orchestra. If you would like to hear how very beautiful the Lim family can play its violin, please come to Bradford Lim's solo recital tonight in Royce Hall. In honor of Kevin's new orchestra, his father have made possible for all Pirelli Youth Orchestra members to be admitted free of charge."

Pirelli threw Kevin a big grin, and the new violinist shifted uncomfortably in his seat. Either the guy was genuinely self-conscious or he had a bad case of heat rash. As I watched him fidget, I noticed someone else who looked even less happy. She was sitting right next to Kevin, and her name was Buffy Dupree.

I thought back to what Splat had told me as we'd walked into the rehearsal hall. He'd whispered confidentially, "Did you know that toads chew with their eyeballs?" Actually, his second comment was more to the point: "I hear Buffy Dupree's really mad because she lost out to Kevin Lim. She's been telling everybody the auditions were fixed."

As I studied Buffy, I could see that Splat's information had been right. She wasn't just looking daggers at Kevin—she was looking shotguns, bazookas, and thermonuclear weapons.

Pirelli tapped the podium with his baton. "And now, ladies and gentlemens, it comes time to begin our very fine week of rehearsals. Each day we shall read through two and three pieces, and as we play, please listen to what the great masters are saying to us. Maybe they say, 'Be brave, peoples of the world.' Maybe they say, 'My heart break with sadness.' These things are between the notes if we listen hard enough."

He shuffled through the musical scores that lay on the podium. "Please to open your folders and take out some special music I am dedicating to our Myron Mann. The piece is call *Till Eulenspiegel's Merry Pranks*, by the great Mr. Richard Strauss. I haven't plan to play this piece until tomorrow, but something tell me to do it first thing this morning." He looked up at Myron, and an impish grin scampered across his swarthy face. "This message was whisper to me by a little bird."

"Actually, it was a bass drum," said Splat.

"We have in this piece," Pirelli continued, "a thing that must be truly amazing. Long ago in Germany, Strauss compose music about a young man who like to play tricks on people. Till Eulenspiegel is his name, but we call him Till. And what instrument plays the part of Till? A French horn, if you would believe it! Now I ask of you, how do Mr. Strauss know about our Myron? I don't have one inkling in the sky. Maybe we can just call it magic—musical magic."

He raised his baton. "Myron, please to look at the beginnings of your music and play this theme for us."

Myron did as he was told, and the rehearsal began. Till's theme was passed from French horn to oboe to clarinet, giving the impression of a prankster scampering through the orchestra. We could hear Till giggling in the woodwinds, dropping water balloons in the strings, and passing out whoopee cushions in the percussion. But in the middle of all the fun, an ominous chord sounded in the low brass. Pirelli signaled for us to stop.

"Now," he said, "what do we hear? As Till play his tricks, the trombones and tuba call out, 'Stop in the name of the law!' Yes, ladies and gentlemens, the police have nab our prankster. They take him to courtside, where the judge give his sentence: He must hang out on the gallows until he die."

I caught Myron's eye. For some reason he didn't seem to be enjoying the story.

"Now, my young friends," said Pirelli, "let us play our music. If you listen close, you can hear what happen."

He gave the downbeat, and the trial began. The low brass issued the judge's pronouncements in a series of stern chords, anchored by Splat's tuba. Till, in the form of a clarinet, pleaded his case desperately, but the judge wasn't buying it. Our muted trumpets marched Till to the gallows, where everything grew quiet. Suddenly two low blasts from Splat and his buddies rang out. The deed was done. In the silence that followed, the woodwinds ushered Till's spirit from his body. The cellos and basses plucked his last few heartbeats, and the violins played a melancholy funeral song. Just about the time I was starting to feel sad, there was a stirring in the percussion. A loud chord in the brass threw open the door, and there was none other than Till, his theme as mischievous as ever. The French horns thumbed their noses at the authorities, and the piece was over.

"They didn't kill him!" called out Mitzi Brody from the flute section.

"You have listen well, Mitzi," said Pirelli, beaming. "Jokes may get us in trouble, as we have see this morning. But the spirit of laughter never die. Isn't this right, Myron?"

Next to me, Myron managed an anorexic smile.

Pleased with himself, Pirelli shuffled the scores on his music stand. "And the hits, they just continue to come! Next we play Mr. George Frideric Handel's most lovely *Water Music* Suite."

Above us, there was a sputtering sound, and a couple of drops fell on my music. The next thing I knew, we were sitting under Niagara Falls.

Somebody had turned on the overhead sprinklers.

2

· · · · · ·

You can tell a lot about people by the way they react in emergencies.

Freddy Fosselman yelled, "Acid rain! Run for your lives!"

Pirelli called out, "Don't let your musics get wet!"

The string players covered up their instruments. The flutists covered up their hair.

"What are we going to do?" shrieked an oboist.

"*Water Music*, I think," said a trombone player, looking up from his paperback novel.

Buffy Dupree produced one of those little fold-up umbrellas from her violin case and calmly gathered up her things.

Splat tap-danced around the room, playing "Singing in the Rain" on his tuba. As he followed the orchestra out of the rehearsal room, he did a little pirouette and murmured, "Gene Kelly, eat your heart out."

Oh, yes, there was one more interesting reaction. Myron Mann laughed. He was still laughing a few minutes later when the sprinklers shut off and Pirelli led his bedraggled troops back into the room.

I clucked my tongue. "You've got to learn to be a little more subtle, My."

"Huh? Hey, do you think I did this?"

"If it's got two eyes on the side of its head and a guitar coming out of its nose, it's a Picasso. If it's seven feet two, wears goggles, and shoots skyhooks, it's a Kareem. The great masters are easy to recognize, My."

"For your information, I had nothing to do with it," he said.

"So why were you laughing?"

He shrugged. "I admire good work, that's all."

Pirelli stepped up to the podium once again. His wig had slipped down over his forehead, and a drop of water dangled from the tip of his nose. As he spoke, he stared straight at Myron. "My young friends, it seem our Merry Prankster is having his fun with us today. But we should remind this person, whose name we don't have one slightest clue of, that some laughs are not funny, and some tricks can be hurting people. And now, if we continue to rehearsing I'm afraid we may sag like some wet noodles. So that's all for this day. Tomorrow maybe we can try less jokes and more musics, okay?"

I packed up my trumpet and, shoes squishing, walked out to the parking lot with Splat. As we made our way across the corner of the UCLA campus where the Pirelli Youth Orchestra rehearsed, a few people stared at our wet clothes.

"Oceanography majors," I told them.

When we got to his car, Splat pulled a drop cloth out of the trunk and spread it across the front seat. "The seat cover's genuine mohair," he said. "If you drip, you die."

I should explain about Splat's car, which is not your usual sort of vehicle. It's the William "Refrigerator" Perry of automobiles. Big and round, it looks like a whale with chrome. In fact, it's a 1949 Packard Custom Eight, with a real wood dashboard, cut-pile carpet, and wool headliner. I know all this because Splat tells me about it every time I get in the car. It's his one obsession in life, other than classical music and acne.

As we climbed in, Splat said, "You'll notice the real wood dashboard, cut-pile carpet . . ."

"Yeah, Splat, I know."

"Just checking."

I should also explain that I don't ride with Splat every day of the week. It's just that my dad's car, an old Hillman named Che Guevara, was at Ollie's Organic Auto Repair being fixed for the third or fourth time that month. Che was there so often, I'd told Dad that Ollie should pay half the license fee.

"I'm hungry," I said as we drove through Westwood.

"The Grand Canyon's big. Birds fly south for the winter. Elmer Fudd needs speech lessons. Tell me something I don't know."

"I'm serious. Hang a right at the golden arch." He

pulled over, and a minute later I was back in the car with a large order of fries and a chocolate shake. I polished them off in a little over two minutes, and we were on our way again.

We headed down Wilshire toward Brentwood, where we'd promised to pick up my dad. He was taking a class of the Free University, a loosely organized school with courses about anything, taught by anyone. A holdover from the sixties, it had originally offered such classes as "A History of Radical Thought in Southeast Asia" and "Storming Barricades 101." My dad's class, held at the home of a Mrs. Zuckerman, was called "Adding Pizzazz to Your Sauces."

"Hi, Sizzle," he said when he climbed into the backseat. "Hey, Splat, how's it going?"

He was a tall, thin man with a shaggy mustache and long hair tied back in a ponytail. Whenever he wasn't dressed in the blue shirt and slacks of the U.S. Postal Service, he wore another uniform: faded jeans and sandals. At a glance it made him look younger than his thirty-six years, but when you looked closer you could make out lines on his forehead and gray streaks in his hair. They'd been there ever since my mom had left in search of a law school and a six-figure income. She'd found both, but in the process had lost touch with a trumpet player and an amateur chef who loved her very much.

My dad opened a plastic container and held it toward us. "This is a wine sauce we whipped up this morning. Dig."

"How about if we tasted it instead?" said Splat.

13

We each dipped a finger in the sauce and tried it. "Hey," said Splat, "this guy's good."

"The best," I said.

My dad closed the container and leaned back, grinning.

"Well, aren't you going to say anything?" I asked, indicating our damp clothes.

"Oh, yeah," he said, "thanks for the compliment."

I reached over and tapped his forehead with my knuckles. "Hello, anybody home?"

"Hey, your hand's wet," he said.

"Dad, Splat and I look like we just took an underwater tour of Sea World. Aren't you curious about what happened?"

"Oh, yeah. What happened?"

I described the morning's events. As I finished, we pulled up to our apartment in Mar Vista, the modest West Los Angeles community where we lived.

"Want to go to that violin recital tonight?" Splat asked me as I got out.

I turned to my dad, and he nodded. "You're on," I told Splat. "Seven thirty?"

"Okeydokey." He pulled the door shut with a thud, and the Packard lumbered off down the street.

I watched it go, then turned toward the apartment building. It was a boxlike, two-story affair that looked more like a motel than an apartment house. The entrances to all the units were on the outside, necessitating an exterior staircase that led to a balcony running the entire length of the second floor. My dad and I climbed the stairs, and he unlocked our front door. When we walked into the darkened apartment, we were confronted with a shadowy form that lay sprawled at our feet. At a glance it appeared to be a dead body, except most dead bodies don't snore and wear flea collars.

I reached down and scratched the body's ear. "Hi, big guy. Rough morning, huh?"

It was my dad's pet basset hound, Mellow, also known as the Haunted Dog. One day he'd be lying by the door, and the next you'd find him stretched out beside the couch. Yet as far as we knew, no one had ever seen him move.

Dad opened the curtains and put on a Charlie Parker album. He liked playing it loud enough so he could absorb the sounds directly through his scalp. Between his records and my practicing, the neighbors had learned to love music whether they liked it or not.

My dad looked at me and his lips moved.

"Why do you always do this?" I said. "You turn the music up, then you try to carry on a conversation."

He walked over and adjusted the volume. "Sorry, Sizzle, but I couldn't hear you. The music was turned up."

"I said— oh, never mind. What did you say?"

"Oh. I was just asking about your date tonight."

"Dad, for the ninety-seventh time, you don't go on 'dates' with Splat. It's more like, I don't know, a lab assignment in biology class where you look at those little wiggly things under the microscope."

"Well, somebody goes on dates with him. I saw him pull up to Chez Pierre last Friday night wearing a coat and tie. There was a girl with him."

"Splat? With a girl? Wearing a tie?"

15

"No, he was wearing the tie."

"Dad, Chez Pierre's one of the fanciest restaurants in town. It couldn't have been Splat."

"He was driving that Packard of his."

I slumped down onto the couch, trying to gather what was left of my wits. It was as if he had told me Billy Graham played the horses, or Clint Eastwood was gay.

"I wonder who that girl was," my dad said.

So did I.

"Prudence! Arthur! Hello, you peoples, hello!" Vidor Pirelli waved at us from across the lobby of UCLA's Royce Hall, where Bradford Lim's violin recital was due to start in just a few minutes.

All around us, people were wearing coats, ties, and dresses. As for the two of us, we had on our usual concertgoing attire: a skirt, blouse, and black Reeboks for me, and jeans and a beat-up leather jacket for Splat. Under the jacket was a T-shirt with the words *Stravinsky was Rite*.

We made our way through the crowd to Pirelli. Indicating the woman at his side, he said, "You have met my dearest dumpling, yes?" Tall and stately, she had olive skin and dark, brooding eyes. She was Pirelli's wife, Carlotta, and she was as unlike a dumpling as any woman I had ever seen.

Carlotta extended her hand, and I grasped it briefly. "Sure," I said. "Good to see you again."

"Charmed, madam," said Splat. He brought her hand to his lips and kissed it.

"Arthur, you nice boy," she purred.

16

"And see who we having right over there," said Pirelli, looking past me. "Young Mr. Kevin Lim and his mother."

Beaming, he motioned them over, and introductions were made all around. Mrs. Lim was a smiling, round-faced woman dressed in a silk evening gown and wearing a corsage. Kevin had on slacks and a blazer.

"Fiddles sounded good this morning," I said to him.

He shrugged and ducked his head. "Thanks."

"Kevin is shy," said Pirelli, "but I will tell you this. Someday he can be every bit as good as his father, believe you me."

"It helps to have your teacher living in the next room," said Mrs. Lim, smiling at her son.

"Free lessons, for one thing," said Splat.

"Yeah, it's great," said Kevin, with a noticeable lack of enthusiasm.

The way he said it made me think it must be hard following in your father's footsteps. Especially if he wears shoes as big as Bradford Lim's.

Pirelli turned to Splat and me. "I want you young peoples to pay special attention to the instrument Mr. Lim play tonight. It is the most famous make of violin, a Stradivarius."

"Wow, a Strad," said Splat. "No kidding?"

At the mention of the violin, Kevin Lim lit up like a neon sign. "Wait till you hear the tone. It's wonderful."

"What's it like to play?" I asked.

Just as suddenly, the neon blinked out. "I don't know," he said.

Mrs. Lim put her arm around her son. There was a

17

pained expression on her face. "The instrument's worth nearly two hundred and fifty thousand dollars. Bradford doesn't allow anyone else to play it."

She excused herself and went with Kevin to find their seats. We did the same. Ten minutes later, Splat and I watched Bradford Lim walk out onto the stage of Royce Hall, carrying a quarter-million bucks' worth of wood and catgut as casually as if it were a Donald Duck lunch pail. As valuable as the violin was, his manner sent a clear message that the most important item on the stage was Bradford Lim himself. This was the man for whom the word *strut* was invented.

Splat leaned over to me. "No wonder Kevin's so shy. With his dad around, there's no room for any more egos."

Lim started off with a Beethoven sonata, then followed with a Mozart, a Brahms, and a Prokofiev. I had to admit the guy was good. Not great, but good. His attacks were clean, his phrasing graceful, and his tone, thanks to the Stradivarius, as thick and rich as maple syrup. There wasn't a single thing you could fault about his playing; and yet I had the distinct feeling that deep down inside the music, something was missing.

"I wonder how good he'd sound without the Strad," I said to Splat as we pulled up to my apartment after the recital.

"It'd be tough. I suppose he could hum."

"Well," I said, getting out of the car, "it's been a barrel of laughs. The only thing funnier would have been if you'd worn a coat and tie."

"I never wear a coat and tie."

"That's not what I hear."

"Huh?"

"Never mind," I said. "See you around."

"Is something bothering you?"

"Not a thing in the world," I said.

I closed the car door and walked off. Behind me, the Packard idled quietly for a few moments. Then it pulled away and drove off down the street.

3
• • • • • • •

Obviously, the thing to do was just forget about it. If Splat wanted to dress up in a monkey suit and take some girl to a fancy restaurant, so what? I wasn't going to grill him about something I didn't even care about. Oh, sure, there was a kind of curiosity, like Pavlov must have felt whenever he saw his dog slobber. But beyond that it really didn't matter to me.

I made a point of riding to Tuesday's rehearsal with Splat just to let him know there was nothing wrong. On the way we stopped off at Del Taco for my minimum daily requirement of vitamins S, G, and C—salt, grease, and cholesterol. As I munched, I noticed two things about Splat. First, he was wearing a T-shirt that said *Opera has been Verdi, Verdi good to me.* Second, he seemed preoccupied.

"A nacho for your thoughts," I said.

"Hmm? Oh, I was just thinking about that Merry Prankster."

"You mean Myron?"

He shrugged. "Or whoever. Myron claims he's innocent."

"Yeah. And Clark Kent's just another skinny guy with glasses."

"I'm going to keep my eyes peeled today," he said.

"Sounds painful."

"I just have a feeling there might be more pranks."

"Hey, come on," I said, "yesterday was probably just an isolated gag. Besides, what could he possibly do for an encore?"

"That's what worries me."

When we arrived at the rehearsal, Splat set up his tuba at the back of the room and began prowling around the halls. I played a few scales and arpeggios and watched as the musicians filed in.

There was Myron Mann, greeting people as though nothing had happened yesterday; Kevin Lim, his face as impassive as Myron's was animated; Buffy Dupree, waiting until the last possible moment to take her place next to Kevin; Harvey Bitner, a hollow-eyed oboist who was never quite satisfied with his reed, his intonation, or the state of the world in general; and Carl Friedlander, our first trombonist, who showed up wearing a raincoat and boots.

As people milled around, Arnie Klingmeyer, the orchestra librarian, handed out the day's music. I felt sorry for Arnie. He was a short, stocky clarinet player who tried out for the orchestra every year and was turned away each time. The musical equivalent of a water boy, he did odd jobs for Pirelli so he could be part of the group. During rehearsals he would stand off to the side with his eyes glued to the woodwind section, fingering the keys of a phantom clarinet.

I glanced at the first piece of music, *Finlandia*, by Jean Sibelius, and wondered what the Merry Prankster could do with this one. Turn on the sprinklers again? Crank up the air conditioner full blast? Build a snowman on the timpani?

Pirelli stepped up to the podium and tapped his baton. "My very young friends, Mr. Jean Sibelius as you know is one of my most favorite composers. I thought we must try today this man's hymn about his country of Finland. As we play, please listen to the rocky shore, the colliding of the waves, and the tall, white peaks in the sky. Also listen between the notes, and you will hear a great love shining through for his peoples. Now come on."

He gave the downbeat, and as we played, the land of Jean Sibelius began to take shape. Fog rolled across the orchestra. A cool breeze blew, and I could swear I smelled seawater. Towering pine trees shot up in the string section. There were fjords in the woodwinds and glaciers in the brass. Pirelli was conducting with his eyes closed, and you could bet he was bopping down some street in Helsinki, checking out the scene.

"And now," he called out over the music, "is coming

up a most lovely tuba note, which may be the rock on which this land is built, or maybe it could be the soul of the Finland peoples."

With his eyes shut Pirelli had no way of knowing that there was one minor problem. The soul of the Finland peoples, a funny-looking kid with zits and a caved-in chest, was still out in the hallway playing detective. As I glanced up, Splat came hurrying back through the door. He had four bars—maybe ten seconds—to make it to his seat.

He sprinted past the violins, bounced off the bass drum, and careened through the horns, pausing next to me long enough to whisper, "The place is clean. No prankster today." He leaped for his chair, grabbed his tuba from its stand, took a deep breath, and, just as Pirelli cued him, blew for all he was worth.

Nothing came out.

Pirelli's eyes popped open. "Now, Arthur, now!"

Splat blew again. His face turned scarlet, and his cheeks puffed up like a couple of red-and-white spotted balloons. This time something came out, but it didn't sound like a tuba. It was more like a drowning hippo, bubbling and gurgling in the key of C-sharp-major.

Pirelli cut us off. "Arthur, what happen to my tuba note?"

"I don't know," Splat said, "but I intend to find out."

He got to his feet and turned his instrument upside down. Out came a few cups of water, followed by a dozen halibut. Or maybe they were mackerel or cod. Whatever they were, they all had fins.

"Welcome to Finland," said Splat.

The Merry Prankster had struck again.

This time the orchestra laughed, and even Pirelli couldn't keep from chuckling a little bit.

"Please, please, Myron," he said, "we beg of you. Enough is too much. You have your fun; now let us play the music, yes?"

Myron just grinned.

"Anybody have some Lysol?" asked Splat.

Pirelli gestured to Arnie Klingmeyer. "Arnie, please to clean up these fishes. And now, ladies and gentlemens, since our Myron have done his last joke for the week, it is time to get down on business. Our next selection will be a chance to hear our new concertmaster play so beautiful for us. Please take out your musics for Mr. Tchaikovsky's most lovely violin concerto."

During the next half hour we found out just how good Kevin Lim was. The kid who seemed so shy in conversation came to life when he had a violin in his hands. The interesting thing was that he was a completely different kind of player from his father. Where his dad exuded confidence and power, Kevin was a portrait of pure joy. In his hands, Tchaikovsky's melodies swooped and soared like a flock of sea gulls. His tone was impeccable, far more beautiful than I'd remembered it from the day before.

We read through the piece just once, but it was enough to convince everyone in the room that we had an all-star in our midst. When Kevin finished the last note, the whole orchestra burst into applause.

"Bravo, Kevin, bravo!" said Pirelli. "We all so proud to have you with us."

Well, maybe not all. As Kevin sat down, Buffy Dupree wore the kind of expression you might see on the local prom queen if Brooke Shields walked into the room.

"And now," said Pirelli, "we play our lasting piece for today. Please turn to Mr. George Frideric Handel's *Royal Fireworks Music.*"

Okay, it was true that for the first time that week we'd gone through an entire musical selection without once hearing from the Merry Prankster. But to my mind, playing this next piece came under the heading of "Why Press Your Luck?"

It wasn't just the title that worried me. I was remembering what we'd learned in music appreciation about its world premiere. It seemed that in 1749 the king of England wanted to put on a big fireworks extravaganza. He hired Handel to write some music, and twelve thousand people showed up to see it.

The music went fine, and then it was time for the fireworks, which included a huge glowing figure of the king. Unfortunately, when they lit the fuse, the king's head burst into flames and crashed to the ground, setting one of the pavilions on fire and causing a stampede in which two people were trampled to death. The royal architect went insane on the spot, drew his sword on the duke of Montagu, and was carried off kicking and screaming.

I hoped Myron wasn't planning anything quite that elaborate.

I glanced over at him and saw that he was wearing a very slight, mischievous grin. "Don't even think it," I told him.

"Think what? Did I do anything?"

"Pure as the driven snow," I marveled.

The music began with the timpani, and I jumped. Every drumbeat and cymbal crash made me sweat. Deep down inside, a little voice kept shrieking, "Look out! Watch it! Duck!"

Pirelli, meanwhile, was off schmoozing with the king of England, blissfully unaware that the fireworks could start any minute.

The funny thing was, they didn't. We went through all six movements without anything unusual happening, unless you count Toby Timmerman dropping pennies down Henrietta Dunn's blouse. When the last note died out, Pirelli grinned, and I shook my head in amazement. No doubt about it. The Merry Prankster had gone bye-bye.

"My young friends," said Pirelli, "see what beautiful things happen when we think about musics instead of banana peels and whoop-de-do cushions. Go home now and think about this."

As I was putting away my trumpet, Splat came by. "Good thing I checked the halls before we started. It must have scared him off."

"Yeah, those fish were the work of a frightened man."

As we headed for the door, I stopped and sniffed the air. "Hey, do you smell something?"

"That's very funny, Sizzle."

"I don't mean the fish. I'm talking about that burning smell."

I glanced around the room, and everything seemed normal. Myron was wandering through the cello section, making wisecracks and flirting with the girls. Arnie Klingmeyer was collecting the music. Harvey Bitner was checking out the bulletin board at the front of the room. Buffy Dupree had packed up her instrument and was walking briskly toward the exit. Vidor Pirelli and Kevin Lim were standing near the podium, chatting.

Suddenly the rehearsal hall was rocked by a series of sharp explosions. It was as if someone were making a batch of cosmic popcorn.

Or setting off firecrackers.

Smoke and flames poured out of Kevin Lim's open violin case. As everyone looked on in horror, Kevin rushed back to his chair and began trying to beat out the fire with his hands.

"Kevin, no!" cried Splat. He raced over and grabbed a fire extinguisher from the wall, then pushed Kevin aside and covered the flames with white foam. By the time I joined him, the place was in an uproar, and Kevin's violin was a smoldering mass of charcoal.

I looked over at Myron Mann. "Great work, My. Just great."

Kevin stood by, dazed. I lifted his hands and looked at them. Blisters were already starting to form.

"We're taking you to the hospital," I told him. "Splat, get your keys."

"I'm not going without my violin," said Kevin. He had an odd, determined look on his face.

"Okay, Kevin," I said. "Sure." I scooped up what was left of his instrument, Splat took his arm, and we hurried off.

"Be careful, peoples," Pirelli called out after us.

As we drove to the hospital, Kevin stared numbly at the violin.

"It's ruined," he kept mumbling.

"Kevin," I said gently, "it's not the end of the world. There are other violins out there."

"Not like this one," he said. "It was my father's Stradivarius."

4
• • • • • • •

As we left the parking lot of the UCLA Medical Center, Kevin Lim was staring at his bandaged hands. I had a hunch what he was seeing was the Stradivarius.

"I'm doomed," said Kevin.

"Come on," said Splat, "it was just a few sticks and some catgut."

"You'll have to pardon my friend," I said. "There are catcher's mitts with more sensitivity."

"Hey, I was just trying to make him feel better," said Splat.

"I've got an hour to figure out what to tell him," Kevin mumbled.

"Your dad?" asked Splat.

"Yeah. He'll be home at one o'clock."

"I know it'll be hard," I said, "but you won't be alone. We'll be right there with you, Kevin."

"Thanks."

"You know," I said to Splat, "what Kevin needs is something deep down inside—something strong, something solid, something dependable to carry him through hard times. In short, what he needs is a Tommy Burger."

"What's that?" asked Kevin.

I glanced at Splat and shook my head sadly. It was hard to believe that the son of an internationally renowned violinist could be so culturally deprived.

"For hikers," Splat explained, "there's Mount Everest. For artists, it's the Louvre. Baseball fans have Wrigley Field, and tourists have Disneyland. For connoisseurs of junk food, such as our friend Prudence here, there's one place and one place only—Tommy's."

"Home of the Tommy Burger," I said in hushed tones.

"I don't know," Kevin said.

"Come on," said Splat. "Your stomach will thank you."

A few minutes later we pulled into the parking lot between a Jaguar and a Mercedes. We ordered three Tommy Burgers and three large Cokes.

I watched Kevin's face as he gingerly picked up the burger in his bandaged hands and took a bite. His cheeks flushed and his eyes began to water. He lifted the top of the bun and looked at what lay beneath. "Onions, tomato . . . and what's this other stuff?"

"Tommy's chili sauce," I replied. "They also use it to clean ship hulls."

30

A few minutes later I finished my burger and looked up at Kevin. He'd barely even touched his.

"Want to talk about it?" I asked.

He shrugged. "I guess."

"What I don't understand," I ventured, "is why you had your dad's violin."

"Yeah," said Splat, "I thought you weren't allowed to play it."

"Today was the first time I ever did. I snuck it out of the house this morning and was going to put it back. He never would have known."

"What if he'd decided to practice?" Splat asked.

"He never even looks at his violin the day after a recital. It's the only time he allows himself a day off."

"But of all the times to borrow it, why did you choose today?" I asked. "Didn't you know it might be risky with all the pranks we've been having?"

"Look," said Kevin miserably, "I know it was stupid. But can you imagine how it feels to practice every day, trying your hardest to improve just a little bit, when you know in the next room there's an instrument that could make you sound twice as good? It's like having a Rembrandt in the house and being told you can't look at it. But today, the timing was perfect. My father wouldn't be practicing, and I was going to play the Tchaikovsky Violin Concerto. How could I pass that up?"

"For what it's worth, Kevin, you sounded great," I said.

"Second the motion," said Splat. "Definitely Juilliard material."

He was referring to the Juilliard School of Music, the top music conservatory in the country. Kevin shook his head.

31

"My father says that's just for the top players. He says I should go to a junior college."

"And you believe him?"

"I'm just not that good," Kevin said.

Splat held a straw up to Kevin's ear and peered through it. "The patient's hearing is normal. But the brain appears hopelessly damaged."

"My father should know," Kevin snapped. "He used to teach at Juilliard. Anyway, even if I had a chance to go there before, I sure don't after today."

He took a few halfhearted bites of his Tommy Burger. "Thanks for bringing me here. But if you guys don't mind, I think I'd better be getting home."

The Lim residence was in Bel Air, an exclusive, gated community where there were more police cars than pedestrians. We parked in the circular driveway and followed Kevin inside. He led us into a den paneled with gleaming mahogany, holding the violin case in his arms as if it were a wounded child.

He walked up to his father, who was lounging in a leather chair next to the stereo system with his eyes closed, wearing earphones.

"Dad," said Kevin. No response. Kevin tapped him on the shoulder.

"Just a minute," said Bradford Lim without opening his eyes. Kevin stood by, waiting.

"Aren't you going to interrupt him?" I whispered.

"Nobody interrupts my father when he's listening to music," Kevin replied.

"What if you were dying?" asked Splat.

He is, I thought.

Lim stood up, took off the earphones, and hung them

on a peg by the chair. He looked at Splat and me, then at Kevin, then at the Stradivarius. Or rather, what used to be the Stradivarius.

He didn't recognize it at first. Then something glimmered in his eye, and his expression began to change. His face grew dark. His mouth tightened, and furrows raked across his forehead. He started breathing harder and harder, like a runner desperate for oxygen.

"There was an accident," said Kevin. He quickly recounted the morning's events.

Lim took the violin and sat down heavily, holding the case in his lap. He kept staring at it, as if looking for signs of life.

There were footsteps behind us. "Kevin, what happened to your hands?" His mother hurried into the den and examined the bandages.

"Just a few minor burns, Mom," said Kevin.

"I told you never to touch this violin," said Lim in a low, dangerous voice.

"The doctor at the hospital told us it wasn't serious," I said.

"Do you know what this instrument was worth?" said Lim.

"Hospital!" cried Kevin's mother.

"A quarter of a million dollars!" said Lim.

"Really, he's fine," I said.

"I know," said Kevin. "I'm sorry. It's all my fault."

"Is anyone else confused?" said Splat.

"Huh?" I said.

"My baby," cooed Kevin's mother.

"My Stradivarius!" bellowed Lim.

The phone rang. Grateful for an interruption, Kevin

hurried over and answered it, holding the receiver gingerly in one bandaged hand. A moment later he hung up.

"That was the police," he said. "Mr. Pirelli called them. They want to see the violin and ask us some questions."

He turned to Splat and me. "Thanks for sticking around. I guess we can handle it from here."

"You got it, Kev," said Splat.

"Let us know when you want to go back to Tommy's," I said.

When we left, Kevin's father was still sitting in his chair, staring at the Stradivarius.

On the way home, Splat said, "Still think Myron's our guy?"

"I don't know. I always thought his taste in practical jokes ran more to banana peels than firecrackers. This doesn't seem like Myron's style."

"Did you notice, though? He was wandering around the string section right before it happened."

"So were at least twenty other people," I said.

"Well, one thing's for sure. We have another mystery on our hands. Don't tell me that doesn't set your tiny heart pounding."

"That doesn't set my tiny heart pounding," I said.

"We're reunited. We're back in the fray. We're in the saddle again."

"Splat, let me explain something. I'm a *me*. You're a *you*. But you and I are not a *we*."

"Don't fight it, Sizzle. We need each other like spaghetti needs meatballs, like polka needs dots. What would Mickey do without Minnie? Where would Gladys Knight be without her Pips?"

"You're saying we're a team?" I asked.

"You got it."

"And team members should never lie to each other, right?"

"Right."

"I understand they have great duck *à l'orange* at Chez Pierre," I said.

"Good for Pierre. Bad for the duck. What's this got to do with teamwork?"

"Look, Splat, I really don't care where you go or who you go with. I just wish you'd tell me the truth."

"Can we start this conversation over? I lost you somewhere between the duck and the orange."

"Okay, fine," I said. "My dad saw you at Chez Pierre last Friday night with some girl."

"Chez Pierre? That expensive French place in Beverly Hills?" He shook his head. "Must have been somebody who looks like me."

"Splat, nobody looks like you."

"I'll take that as a compliment."

"Don't change the subject, smart guy."

"You want the truth?"

"Yup."

"No apologies, no punches pulled? Raw, naked, unvarnished?"

"That's right."

"The truth," said Splat, "is that last Friday night I spent a quiet evening with my mother. I don't know how raw that is, but I swear there's not a drop of varnish on it."

5

• • • • • • •

Arthur Hadley Reavis Pauling III was many things: wise guy, nerd, car enthusiast, bug collector, comic book freak, tuba jock, and dermatologist's nightmare. But in all the time I'd spent with him, I'd never known him to be a liar. So the Chez Pierre business had me confused.

Could it be Splat was telling the truth? If so, who or what had my dad seen that night in Beverly Hills? If Splat was lying, what was he trying to cover up? And most puzzling of all, why was I suddenly talking like the narrator in a low-budget detective movie?

Splat picked me up the next morning wearing a T-shirt that said *Haydn go seek*, and we drove to the rehearsal in silence. When we arrived, Vidor Pirelli looked like he had slept on a park bench. Clothes wrinkled, face unshaven, wig askew, he stumbled into the rehearsal hall at nine thirty. He went directly to the podium, where he faced a room that was half-empty.

"I am so very sorry I'm late for today's rehearsal, my young friends," he said. "I haven't sleep well all night because of yesterday's terrible accident."

He glanced at Kevin Lim's empty chair. "You will all be happy to know that our Kevin is fine. His hands were burn some little bit, but thanks to Arthur and Prudence there is nothing serious."

He nodded in our direction and gave us a tired smile. "I have talk to Kevin this morning," Pirelli continued, "and he will be playing his violin again very soon."

I'd talked to Kevin, too. He might start playing again soon, but he wouldn't be doing much of anything else for a long time. His father had grounded him for a month.

"But while Kevin is out," Pirelli continued, "we have a wonderful replacement for him with our very fine Miss Buffy Dupree."

Buffy deigned to give us one of her haughty smiles, the kind Marie Antoinette must have given the peasants right before she gave them permission to eat cake.

"I see," said Pirelli, "that many of our orchestra members are not with us today. Their mothers and fathers perhaps are scared of new tricks which might be play. And, ladies and gentlemens, I must be telling you that so am I. I have been thinking about this all through last night, and this morning I am here before you to say that we are finish with our rehearsals for this week."

There were groans from the remaining orchestra members. I noticed that Buffy in particular didn't look too happy. Pirelli held up his hand. "I know you must be disappointed, my friends, but we cannot play our lovely musics when it might blow up in our hand at any minute. So please, go home. There will be no more musics this week. But there will be no more tricks either."

Wrong.

He stepped off the podium, and as we began putting our instruments away he walked over to his office. When he opened the door, pigeons flew out.

It seemed as if there were thousands, though in retrospect there were probably just forty or fifty. They streamed past an astonished Pirelli and headed for the wild blue yonder. Finding none, they wheeled and circled the perimeter of the room over and over again, looking for a way out.

The rest of us simply stood there staring with our mouths open. Which, as it turned out, was not the smartest thing to do.

"Dive bombers three o'clock high!" yelled Freddy Fosselman.

Tiny projectiles rained down on us from overhead. Appropriately enough, the first person to be struck was Splat.

"Medic, medic!" cried Freddy.

"Yuck!" said Mitzi Brody, the second victim. "My brand-new sweater!"

"They're bombing women and children!" Freddy shouted.

It was at that point when people started ducking for cover, some under instrument cases, others beneath music stands and chairs. The coolest of the bunch was Buffy

Dupree, who once again had produced an umbrella from nowhere.

I hurried over to the emergency exit leading outside and threw open the door. Then I grabbed some sheet music from the percussion section, stood on a chair next to the door, and waved the music to divert the pigeons through the exit. They whizzed past me, and for a moment I felt like some sort of demented traffic cop.

I followed the last few birds out the door and watched as they circled the area a few times then flew due west. When I went back inside, the entire orchestra was on its feet, applauding.

I gave them a mock bow. "Once again, saved by music," I proclaimed, holding up the percussion part. As I did, I happened to glance at it.

If the rehearsal hadn't been called off, the piece we would have been playing was Holst's *The Planets*. The name of the first section caught my eye.

" 'Mercury, Winged Messenger,' " I read. I looked over at Myron Mann. "You don't know when to quit, do you?"

"Sizzle, I didn't do it. I swear to God, I didn't do any of this stuff."

"Yeah, right." I gave the music back to the percussionists and turned to Arnie Klingmeyer. "Arnie, get us some paper towels, huh? Let's clean this place up."

"I hate to even mention it," said Splat, "but I wonder what Pirelli's office looks like. The birds must have been in there quite a while."

As it turned out, they'd made the most of their time. What we found was the world's first polka-dot office, stocked with enough feathers to outfit several teams of pillow fighters. And there was something else: a pigeon, with one leg tied to the chair so it couldn't fly away with the others.

"Hey," said Splat, "there's a strip of paper on its leg."

"Something tells me we've found our winged messenger," I said.

I picked up the bird and held it while Splat removed and unfolded the paper. On it was a message written in letters cut from a magazine.

> Pigeons are gray.
> Pranks are fun.
> You can relax now,
> Because I'm all done.
> The Merry Prankster

"Shakespeare he's not," said Splat.

"But he's smart," I said. "There's no handwriting or even a typewriter to trace."

Splat tucked the message into his pocket and looked at the pigeon, which was still nestled snugly in my hands.

"Have you noticed how tame that bird is?" he said.

I nodded. "It's a trained racing pigeon. I used to know a woman who owned some of these."

I walked out of the office and through the open emergency door, with Splat right behind me. Outside, I opened my hands, and the pigeon fluttered up into the sky and flew off.

When we came back inside, Arnie had brought some towels, and everyone was busy cleaning up. Everyone, that is, except Buffy Dupree. She was in Pirelli's office using the phone. When she saw we were looking at her, she said a quick good-bye, picked up her violin case, and walked briskly out the door.

"Did that seem strange to you?" said Splat.

"Yeah, a little. So?"

"Let's follow her."

"You love that detective stuff, don't you?" I said.

"Hey, we're on a case. Are you in or not?"

"Following Buffy Dupree to her manicurist does not constitute a case."

Splat looked at me, waiting.

Finally I shrugged. "Okay, I'm in."

We hurried down the hall and emerged from the building. Straight ahead of us, Buffy Dupree was sprinting toward the parking lot.

"Boy, those nails must be in terrible shape," said Splat.

"So she's in a hurry. That doesn't make her guilty."

I had to admit, though, watching Buffy Dupree run was a remarkable sight, roughly equivalent to seeing Princess Di crawl under the royal limousine to give it a quick oil change and lube.

We cut over behind some shrubs and, out of Buffy's line of sight, made our way quickly to the Packard. When we pulled out, another car was just leaving the lot.

"It's amazing," I said. "I've never seen Buffy's car, but one glance and I knew for sure that was it."

"Yeah," said Splat, "you don't see that many shocking pink BMWs."

She sped through Westwood and hopped onto the freeway, where she zigzagged over to the fast lane. We managed to keep her in view while staying a comfortable distance behind. A few minutes later she veered suddenly to the right and took the Santa Monica Freeway downtown.

"And so," said Splat, "they turned east, feeling themselves drawn inexorably toward the dark underbelly of Los Angeles."

"Do you always narrate while you're driving?"

"Only during high-speed car chases involving harebrained violinists."

"By the way," I said, "I've always been curious—what's an underbelly?"

"The opposite of an overbelly."

Urban anatomy notwithstanding, Buffy whizzed right past the downtown exits and headed toward Pasadena.

"I don't get it," said Splat. "Pasadena doesn't even have an underbelly."

He was wrong. When Buffy got off the freeway we found ourselves driving between rows of old warehouses and commercial structures dating back fifty years or more. After several blocks Buffy turned down an alley. Not wanting to be seen, we left the Packard on the street and peered around the corner of a building into the alley.

Buffy had parked her car and, violin case in hand, was knocking on a rickety, unmarked door. As we watched, it opened and she slipped inside.

"Wow," said Splat. "Real cloak-and-dagger stuff."

"Yeah, but what have we really learned?"

"Nothing, yet. Come on." He started into the alley. With my heart somewhere up around my uvula, I followed.

We crept up near the door and paused a moment, trying to decide what to do next. As we waited, we heard muffled voices coming from inside. One was Buffy's, and the other sounded like an older man's. It was impossible to make out exactly what they were saying, but we did hear the words *pigeon* and *mess*. And there was something else. Buffy was laughing.

The voices buzzed on for a while, then a violin began to play. Splat gestured for us to go, and we retreated back down the alley.

"Still think Myron Mann is our prankster?" he asked as we stood in front of the building.

"I wouldn't rule him out."

"Don't you think the old Bufferoo's been acting a little strange lately?"

I shrugged. "What do you expect from someone who drives a pink BMW?"

"Think about it, Sizzle. Who raced across town to talk about pigeons in Pasadena? Who was the only person in the orchestra who just happened to have an umbrella handy when the sprinklers went on? Who pulled out that very same umbrella when the pigeons started dive bombing? And get this—who takes over as concertmaster with Kevin Lim out?"

"Yeah, I suppose. But it's hard to imagine Buffy Dupree tampering with sprinklers or wrestling with pigeons. And what about the *Finlandia* prank? I can't see her dealing with raw fish anywhere outside a sushi bar."

"Maybe she has an accomplice. Like the guy inside that building."

"But who is he?" I asked. "And why would he care?"

Splat walked over and checked the mailbox. "He's either Tidy Room Cleaning Service, Arnie and Bruce Interiors, Gomez and Greenberg—Attorneys-at-Law, or somebody named Giuseppe Cantini."

"Cantini . . . that name sounds familiar."

"It's a pasta dish, isn't it?"

"He has something to do with music," I said. "Come on, let's go talk to somebody who'd know."

"And who would that be?"

"Vidor Pirelli."

6
· · · · · · ·

Vidor Pirelli sat in his office, which after several hours of scrubbing, rubbing, and spraying had been restored to something like its original condition. Outside, the last few orchestra members were finishing the cleanup of the rehearsal room.

"Giuseppe Cantini?" he said. "Of course. He is some very fine violin teacher."

"Does he teach Buffy Dupree, by any chance?" I asked.

"Yes, I believe. Also some other peoples in our orchestra."

I looked over at Splat. "So much for your theory. Buffy was on her way to a lesson."

"Weaving in and out of traffic at seventy miles an hour?"

"So she's a lousy driver. Mr. Pirelli, I have another question for you. What made you decide to play *Till Eulenspiegel's Merry Pranks* at that first rehearsal?"

"I love this jolly piece. I had planned to play it from several weeks ago."

"You planned it before you knew anything about the pranks?" asked Splat.

"Yes, that's right."

"Then your decision to play *Till Eulenspiegel* must have given somebody the idea of becoming the Merry Prankster," I said. "That's the only thing that makes sense. Otherwise it's too much of a coincidence."

"Of course!" said Splat. "So if Mr. Pirelli gives us a list of people who knew what music we'd be playing, one of the names would have to be the Merry Prankster. Sizzle, that's great!"

"This all make good sense," said Pirelli, "except for one small thing. I have told only one person which musics we are playing."

"Perfect," I said. "What's his name?"

"Wait a minute, don't tell us," said Splat. "It was Buffy Dupree, right?"

A strange expression crossed Pirelli's face. "Buffy? No, of course not. I am speaking of Arnie Klingmeyer."

Arnie Klingmeyer and his mother lived in a pink stucco apartment building called Tahiti Village, though as far as I could tell, the only thing Tahitian about it was a wilted palm tree next to the trash cans. When we walked up to the front door we heard strange noises coming from inside. Quite obviously there was a brutal crime taking place. Arnie was murdering Mozart.

He came to the door carrying the murder weapon, a clarinet. "Hi, guys," he said happily. "I was just practicing the Mozart Clarinet Concerto. Maybe I can play it for you sometime."

"Uh, sure, Arnie," said Splat.

"Actually," I said, "we're here about something else. Could we come in for a minute?"

"Huh? Yeah, of course. Are you kidding?"

Grinning, he held open the door, and we walked into a dimly lit room. The curtains were drawn, so the only light came from a portable TV in the corner. By its glow we could see a heavyset woman seated on the couch with a cigarette dangling from her mouth.

When we walked in, she snuffed out her cigarette and looked up from the TV, smiling crookedly. "That Wink Martindale's something, isn't he?"

"Mom," said Arnie, "this is Sizzle and Splat."

"Sizzle? Splat? What kinds of names are those?"

"Onomatopoeic," said Splat.

"They're friends of mine from the orchestra," Arnie said.

"Tell me," she asked us, "do you kids get to play, or are you part of the backup squad like Arnie here?"

"Oh, we play," said Splat. "I'm tuba. Sizzle's trumpet."

"You know," she said, "my Arnie practices for two hours every day after school. He skips baseball, he skips movies—all he does is practice. Every year he tries out for that orchestra, and every year they turn him down. In my book that's wrong."

"Mom, please," said Arnie.

I groped for something to say. "Gee, Mrs. Kling-meyer, Arnie's a very important part of the orchestra. He orders the music and hands it out. He does all kinds of things."

"Well, I'm not happy about it," she said. "And neither is Arnie, but he'd never tell you that."

"Sizzle, would you guys like to come back to my room?" said Arnie, moving toward the doorway.

"Yeah, sure," I answered, following him.

"So long, Mrs. Klingmeyer," said Splat.

She turned back to the TV.

Arnie's room was a small, sparsely furnished place. There was a music stand in the middle with a chair in front of it. But the thing you noticed most was the walls. They were lined with pictures of the Pirelli Youth Orchestra.

"The orchestra really means a lot to you, doesn't it?" I said.

He nodded. "I've wanted to join ever since I was in junior high. I figure if I practice enough, someday I'll make it."

I thought about the dozens of kids I knew who had taken up an instrument because their parents had forced them to, or because there happened to be a violin or flute that had been handed down in the family—kids who had never tried very hard or cared very much and yet had turned out to be pretty good. Then I thought of Arnie Klingmeyer sitting alone in his room practicing hour after hour, preordained by some quirk of genetics to sound more like a duck than a clarinet player, and for a moment I felt some of the anger and frustration Arnie must have felt.

"Your mom said you're not happy being librarian," I said. "Is that true?"

He shrugged. "It's better than not being in the orchestra at all."

"Doesn't it ever bother you to pass out all that music and know you won't be playing it?" asked Splat.

Arnie looked down and mumbled something.

"Sorry, I didn't hear you," I said.

"I said yes, it bothers me, okay?" He looked up. "I do a lot more than just pass out music. I order it, too. Sometimes I even help Mr. Pirelli decide what pieces to play."

"How about *Till Eulenspiegel*?" asked Splat. "Did you help pick that out?"

Arnie walked over to a picture of the Pirelli Youth Orchestra and gazed at it for a few moments. Then he turned back to Splat.

"Look, I may not be a great clarinet player, but that doesn't mean I'm stupid. I know what you're thinking. I didn't pick out that piece, and I didn't have anything to do with those pranks."

"But you knew what we'd be playing this week," I said.

"Of course I did. I'm the one who ordered the music. But I wasn't the only one who knew."

"You weren't?"

"There's always one or two people who borrow music ahead of time so they can practice their parts. Come to think of it, this week there were more than usual."

"Like who, for instance?" I asked.

"Myron Mann. Harvey Bitner. Kevin Lim, so he could work on the Tchaikovsky concerto. Then Buffy Dupree came by, and I had to make a copy of it for her. All of them saw the names of the pieces we'd be playing this week."

"So they not only knew about *Till Eulenspiegel,*" said Splat, "but about *Finlandia,* the *Water Music,* and everything else?"

"That's right. I guess that makes them suspects, huh?"

"We suspect everyone, and we suspect no one," said Splat.

"What does that mean?" Arnie asked me.

"It means he's been watching too many Charlie Chan movies. Come on, Splat, we've got work to do."

"We've been pussyfooting around long enough," I said when we got into the car. "Let's get down to the nuts and bolts of this case."

"Nuts? You want to go see Myron?"

"Not yet. First we talk to Shadrack Holmes."

"Wow, is this guy a detective?" asked Splat.

"Not exactly."

We drove to the UCLA campus and parked near the music building. Around the back on the basement level was an office few people knew about and still fewer visited. On the door was a hand-lettered sign that said *Shadrack Holmes, M.D.* I knocked.

"He's a doctor?" said Splat.

Before I could answer, the door was opened by a middle-aged black man who wore neatly pressed khaki slacks and shirt and carried a ring of keys on his belt.

"Sizzle!" he said, smiling warmly. "How you been?"

"Still blowing," I said.

"Who's your friend?"

"Splat."

"Yeah, but what's his name?"

50

"I'm going to ignore that," said Splat, extending his hand. "Speaking of names, you're no Tom, Dick, or Harry yourself."

Grinning, Shadrack clasped Splat's hand. "That's true, too. My name's from the Bible."

"So's mine," said Splat. "It's the sound Goliath made when he stepped on the Israelites."

"Hey, I like this guy," said Shadrack.

"He grows on you," I said. "Kind of like a fungus."

"So, you're an M.D.?" asked Splat.

"That's right—maintenance director," replied Shadrack. "You know, what they used to call janitor. Hey, what kind of host am I? You guys want to come in? Sizzle, I got your favorite."

A few minutes later we were settled in his office, munching on Cheetos.

"God, I love these," I said.

"They look like worms," said Splat.

Shadrack reached for the cupboard. "I can get you something else if you want."

"Actually, I like worms," said Splat.

"We didn't just come by for a snack," I said. "We wanted to ask you something."

"You mean about that Merry Prankster?" said Shadrack. He chuckled when he saw our looks of surprise. "Hey, this is the craziest thing that's happened around here for years. What kind of maintenance director would I be if I didn't know about it?"

"I was just wondering about those sprinklers in the ceiling," I said. "How do you think the prankster set those to go off?"

"I'm glad somebody's interested," he said. He opened

a drawer in his desk and pulled out an electric timer. It was the kind you buy at the hardware store to turn your lights on and off while you're out of town. "I found this hooked up to the sprinkler system the day after your little shower. Mr. Prankster short-circuited the wiring and hooked up this timer. He set it to turn on the sprinklers at ten thirty and turn them off again five minutes later. I showed it to that police fellow, but he didn't seem to care."

"What police fellow?" I asked.

"The one who came down when Mr. Pirelli reported the firecracker business. Funny sort of guy. It was sunny outside, and he was wearing a trench coat."

"His name wasn't Denton, was it?" I asked.

"There you go."

Splat looked at me. "Niles Denton. My favorite detective."

"Shadrack," I said, "you've seen what the prankster did. Do you get any feel for who this person could be?"

He scratched his chin. "I don't know, Sizzle. Sprinklers. Fish. Firecrackers. Pigeons. Everything he does is so different, it's hard to get a feel for the man."

"Or woman," said Splat.

"One thing," Shadrack said. "They'd have to be good with their hands—you know, mechanical-like."

"So much for Buffy," I said. "Her idea of mechanical is an electric curling iron."

"She could have had help from Cantini," said Splat.

"Cantini," mused Shadrack. "Isn't that some kind of pasta dish?"

"Thanks, Shadrack," I said. "You're a gentleman, a

scholar, and a maintenance director. Plus you have great taste in junk food."

He grinned. "Come back any time. You too, Split."

"Splat."

"Whatever."

7

• • • • • • •

He had a smirk on his face, a cigarette behind his ear, and a portrait of Bogey on the wall. His name was Niles Denton, and in his own mind he was a throwback to the days when detectives liked their coffee black and their facts straight. In my mind he was a twenty-five-year-old kid in a baggy raincoat and a funny hat who'd been reading too many Raymond Chandler novels.

"You again?" he said when we walked into his office at the West L.A. police station.

"Just thought we'd drop in and say hello," I told him.

"Hello," said Splat.

"Why is it," I said, "that everybody else in this place

has new furniture, and you end up with a metal desk and a bare light bulb?"

Denton sighed. He took the cigarette from behind his ear, struck a match with his thumbnail, and lit up. "Look, Szyznowski, I know why you're here. Save yourselves some time and forget it."

"That's what you said last time," said Splat.

"Last time" had been a few months before, when Splat and I had solved a kidnapping in the orchestra. Denton, heading up the investigation for the police, had refused to take us seriously until the day we deposited the kidnapper on his doorstep, wrapped up with a bow.

"Beginner's luck," he muttered. Cigarette or no, he suddenly reminded me of a kid who'd just lost a game of Monopoly. "Besides, this case is different. It's not a case at all. It's just a practical joke that got out of hand."

"Expensive joke," I said.

He nodded. "I saw the violin, or what was left of it. In fact, we have it here at the station. I figured we'd hang on to it for a week or so in case anything else came up."

"Why weren't you interested in the timer on the sprinklers?" I asked.

"Huh? Oh, that. You must have talked to the janitor."

"Maintenance director," said Splat.

"Yeah, he showed me the timer," said Denton, "but by that time I knew it didn't matter. The only reason the police were called in was because the Stradivarius was destroyed, and that was just bad luck. The Lim kid picked the wrong day to borrow daddy's fiddle, that's all."

"Doesn't that seem like quite a coincidence?" I said.

"Not when you've been in this business as long as I have," said Denton.

"Which must be, what . . . two, three hours by now," said Splat, glancing at his watch.

"Coincidences happen every day," said Denton. "That's what people don't realize. Half the cases I work on involve luck of one kind or another."

"Especially if they're solved," said Splat.

"Keep it up, wise guy," said Denton. He took a drag from his cigarette and sent what was supposed to be a smoke ring floating up toward the ceiling. It looked more like an amoeba doing the bump and grind.

"Maybe you're right about it being a coincidence," I said.

"He is?" said Splat.

"But," I said, "that doesn't mean it was an accident."

"You're talking in riddles," wheezed Denton.

"Okay," I said, "let's say I'm the prankster. I know in advance we're going to play the *Royal Fireworks Music*, so I have a string of firecrackers to set off during the piece—just a joke, you understand, like the sprinklers or the fish. But before that, Kevin Lim gets up and plays the Tchaikovsky Violin Concerto, and he doesn't just sound good. He sounds like Heifetz in tennis shoes. Let's say I'm bitter to start with—maybe that's the reason I'm playing all these pranks in the first place—and when I hear that concerto, suddenly I find myself getting so jealous I can hardly stand it. So at the last minute I change my plans and decide to slip the firecrackers into Kevin's violin."

"Not that I'm buying this," said Denton, "but just for the sake of argument, do you know it's a Stradivarius?"

"Yeah, maybe I do. Maybe I saw the Strad at Bradford Lim's recital the night before. Then when Kevin sounded so great this morning I put two and two together and got two hundred and fifty thousand. Now I've got a shot at the prank to end all pranks, and all I have to do is light the fuse."

Splat was leaning forward, excitement scrawled across his face. "So the fact that Kevin brought the Strad was pure luck, but destroying it was no accident."

"Right. It's a coincidence, but it's still a crime."

Denton shook his head. "Nice try, Szyznowski, but you're overlooking something. If this is the prank to end all pranks, why bring out the pigeons the next day? It doesn't make sense. It's unnecessary."

"Maybe that's why the prankster did it," I said. "To throw us off the scent."

Denton settled back in his chair. "Give me a break."

"It makes more sense than what you're saying," Splat shot back. "According to your scenario, the prankster's just an innocent person playing tricks for fun, right?"

Denton nodded, trying his best to look bored.

"Okay, so one day a prank backfires, destroying an instrument worth a quarter of a million bucks and sending someone to the hospital. Don't you think your innocent person's going to lay off for a while?"

"Not necessarily. Kids do funny things."

"So do police detectives," Splat muttered. "Come on, Sizzle, let's go."

"Look," I said to Denton as we headed for the door,

"we just want to solve this thing, and we were hoping you did, too."

"Jokes don't have solutions, Szyznowski. They only have punch lines."

As we left the police station, the sun was dipping behind the billboards and palm trees.

"Well, somebody's got to solve this case," said Splat. "Still game?"

I thought of the look on Kevin's face when he saw what was left of his father's violin. "Count me in," I said.

That night after dinner I made a call to an old friend.

"Hi, Mrs. Fram, remember me?"

"Sugar Ray Szyznowski! I'd recognize that voice anywhere."

"It's been a few years. Still driving the school bus?"

"Yeah, but it hasn't been the same since you graduated. You knew how to keep 'em in line, Sugar Ray."

"I just didn't like seeing big kids pick on little kids, that's all."

"Too bad they don't allow girls in the Golden Gloves. You had a sweet left hook."

"I've sort of outgrown that, Mrs. Fram. These days I try to use words instead of brute force."

"On the other hand, there's nothing like a swift kick in the butt to get a point across."

"Actually, Mrs. Fram, I called to ask you about something."

"Let 'er rip."

"Do you still race pigeons?"

"Sure. You know, I've had three husbands, eight children, seven dogs, and hundreds of pigeons leave home. The pigeons are the only ones that ever came back."

"Are you in a pigeon club or anything?"

"You bet. Want to join?"

"No thanks. I was just wondering, have you heard anything recently about stolen pigeons?"

"Who'd be dumb enough to steal pigeons? They'd fly right back to their owner."

"Just think for a second, Mrs. Fram. Are you sure?"

"Now that you mention it, old Benny was muttering something at the meeting last night. Said he went out back and his cage was empty. 'Course, some of us think Benny's cage has been empty for a long time."

"Did the pigeons ever come back?"

"Well, I saw him again today and he said they were back. Personally, I figured Benny had one too many snorts of Geritol."

"Can you give me his address?"

"You bet, Sugar Ray. But if you're going to visit him, be careful."

"Why's that?"

"Benny says there's a six-foot pigeon that lives in the front yard."

There was no sign of the pigeon, but there were plenty of weeds. They grew in great bunches from the sidewalk to the porch and were almost tall enough to hide the rusted auto parts.

"Not much of a house," Splat said as we emerged from the car into the midmorning sun. "Nice yard, though."

We shouldered our way to the porch and knocked on the screen door. When no one came, I knocked louder.

"Hello, Benny?" I called.

A few seconds went by, then a raspy voice answered, "I'm over here. Follow my voice. This way."

We left the porch and walked over to the side of the house, where we saw a man with tiny, incandescent eyes and the tallest cowlick I had ever seen. He was wearing a faded blue suit with a hole in the knee and was talking with his hands cupped around his mouth.

"A little to your right. No, left, left. Now straight ahead. You're doing fine."

"We're right in front of you, Benny," I said.

He waved his hand in the air. "Here I am."

"We know," I said.

"Oh. Hello there. Did you have any trouble finding me?"

"Not a bit," I said. "Good directions."

"I was in back talking to my pigeons," he said.

"How are they?" asked Splat.

"Fine, fine. You know, it's an interesting thing about pigeons. The only language they really understand is Spanish. Luckily, I studied it in school. *Gusto con bien,* know what I mean?"

"Funny," said Splat, "I would have figured them for pigeon English."

"Benny," I said, "we were given your name by a friend of mine, Mrs. Fram."

"They talk back to me, too," Benny said. "In Spanish, of course."

"Of course," said Splat.

"Here, I'll show you what I mean." Benny led us into a backyard dominated by a huge walk-in cage made of two-by-fours and chicken wire. Inside, dozens of gray pigeons warbled softly to themselves.

"See?" said Benny. "Spanish."

"That's amazing," said Splat.

Benny walked up to the cage. "*Hasta laredo, mu-chandos.*"

The pigeons went on about their business, which mostly involved a lot of sitting and staring.

Benny translated. "They say they're happy to see me and want to know who my new friends are."

"Prudence Szyznowski," I said. "And Arthur Pauling."

"Tell them we come in peace," said Splat.

Benny faced the pigeons. "*Los nuevos manos vendetta placebo.*" He listened for a moment, then nodded in satisfaction.

"Could you ask them something for me?" I said.

"You bet, *señoranda.*"

"Ask them where they disappeared to the other day."

"How'd you know about that?" he said.

"Mrs. Fram told me. We were talking about pigeons because there were some at our youth orchestra rehearsal yesterday."

"Couldn't have been mine," said Benny. "These birds flew to Tijuana to visit relatives. Told me so themselves. Funny you should mention a youth orchestra, though. My next door neighbor's kid's in one of those. Maybe you know him—Myron Mann."

Standing in the doorway, Myron's mother looked perfectly normal except for one small detail.

"I hope you don't mind my asking," I said, "but is there some reason you're wearing a rubber arrow through your head?"

"Myron's little sister Susie likes me to wear it," Mrs. Mann answered in a tired voice. "She says it makes her laugh. Then again, most things make her laugh."

"Runs in the family, I guess," said Splat.

"It's a disease, like the heartbreak of psoriasis. They get it from their father."

"Wow, I didn't know Myron had skin problems," said Splat.

She sighed. "Another comedian. It's the story of my life."

"Is Myron around?" I asked her.

She shook her head. "You could probably catch up with him tonight at the Snickers Bar. It's a comedy club for teenagers. Myron has a lease on a corner booth."

"Thanks," I said, "we'll check it out."

As we turned to go, I stopped. "Mrs. Mann, have you noticed Myron doing anything unusual this past week?"

"Let's see. He put a rubber olive in his father's martini. He lined my slippers with Vaseline. He taped a picture of Godzilla to Susie's mirror. But no, nothing unusual."

8
• • • • • • •

It was a little after nine o'clock when we arrived at the Snickers Bar. We paid at the door and were directed to Myron's booth, where we found our Mann talking to a young woman with sad eyes and a nose the size of the Goodyear blimp.

He looked up. "Sizzle, Splat!"

"You do and you'll clean it up," said the young woman.

"What brings you guys here?" asked Myron.

"Mystery, intrigue, romance," said Splat.

"A Packard," I said.

Myron nodded toward the young woman. "I'd like

you guys to meet a friend of mine, Lucinda Lust. She's a comic."

Lucinda dabbed at her nose with a napkin. "Stage name. I do a kind of post-feminist psychosexual thing in my act."

"Has them rolling in the aisles," said Myron.

"I can imagine," said Splat.

We sat down and ordered a couple of root beers. Up onstage, a kid who looked like captain of the audiovisual squad was doing sound effects with his mouth. He did a Beverly Hills garbage truck and a duck with hay fever, but the audience wasn't buying it.

"Brutal," murmured Lucinda.

"Flop sweat," said Myron.

"Pardon me?" I said.

"Flop sweat," said Myron. "It's what you break into when you're dying onstage, like Sammy up there."

It reminded me of a solo I'd once played with the Pirelli Youth Orchestra. Which in turn reminded me of why we were there.

"Myron," I said, "we had a chat with your next-door neighbor this morning."

"Benny?" he answered a little too casually. "Nice guy."

"His pigeons are nice, too," said Splat. "But the other day they disappeared for no apparent reason. Benny thinks they went to Tijuana. We think they went someplace closer."

"Did I miss something?" Lucinda asked.

"I don't know anything about it, okay?" said Myron.

"Sorry, My," said Splat, "but your eyes are telling a different story."

"A valuable instrument was destroyed and someone was hurt," I said. "This is no joke, Myron."

"What are you guys, cops in training?" said Lucinda.

"Okay," Myron blurted, "I'll tell you the truth, but you're not going to believe me. Yesterday Benny told me about his pigeons disappearing. Just like you, I figured they were the ones at our rehearsal."

"Why didn't you tell somebody?" I asked.

"You think I'm nuts? Most people already think I'm guilty. This would have cinched it."

"So you're saying it's just a coincidence the missing pigeons live right next door to you?" I asked.

"No. I'm saying somebody planned it to make me look bad."

Splat studied Myron thoughtfully. "Sizzle, do you notice anything about Myron? A gleam on the forehead, a little moisture on the upper lip?"

I nodded. "Flop sweat."

"I was just thinking," Splat said later in the car.

"Oxymoron," I said.

"Are you calling me a fat dunce?"

"An oxymoron is a self-contradicting statement," I said. "It's a term in logic."

"You want logic? I'll give you logic. Shadrack Holmes told us the prankster is good with his hands. Arnie Klingmeyer gave us a list of people who had the music ahead of time. Who's the one person we haven't considered who qualifies on both counts?"

I thought about it for a second. "Of course. Why didn't I think of him?"

"Because," said Splat, "you're an oxymoron."

It was noon Friday when we approached a rickety apartment building in Culver City. I was wearing a tank top and shorts, and Splat had a T-shirt with the words *Brahms away!* written across the front. When I knocked at the door, it was opened by a gaunt young man with hollow cheeks and hooded eyes. It was Harvey Bitner. As usual, he was carrying a knife.

"How's it going, Harvey?" I said.

"Terrible. What do you want?"

"Got a second to talk?"

He grunted and motioned us in. We entered a tiny one-room apartment with a bed in one corner and a hot plate in another. In the middle of the floor were a card table and a wooden chair. Two oboes lay across the table, and next to them were wire, string, needle-nose pliers, and several pieces of cane about a quarter inch across. Harvey flopped into the chair, picked up one of the pieces, and started whittling with that most important tool of the reedmaker's trade, the knife.

"It's not fair, you know," he said without looking up. "Brass players don't have to drill their own mouthpieces. String players don't build their own bows. Percussionists don't make anything but noise. So why is it that oboe players are forced to spend their entire lives carving reeds?"

Splat shrugged. "Obviously it's a plot."

"Sometimes I wonder," said Harvey.

"Come on, admit it," I said. "Secretly you enjoy working on reeds."

I figured it would get a reaction, and it did. "Oh, yeah, I enjoy it. I love spending an hour on a reed to get it just the way I want, knowing it's only going to last two weeks. I love going into a big concert scared to death my reed's going to conk out in the middle of a solo."

"How do you really feel about it, Harv?" asked Splat.

Harvey turned an icy gaze on him. "You people are so smug. String players, brass players, all you have to worry about is the music."

"You sound jealous," I said.

"Maybe I am."

"Brass and string players have their own problems, Harvey," I said. "After all, there's no such thing as the perfect instrument."

"If there were, Harvey'd probably want to smash it," said Splat. "Right, Harv?"

"Hmm," said Harvey, deep into his work.

"Some people say there is a perfect instrument," said Splat. "It's a Stradivarius."

Harvey looked up, alarmed. "Wait a minute."

"Jealousy," said Splat. "Now there's a good old-fashioned motive."

"You think I had something to do with that accident?" asked Harvey.

"You were hanging around the front of the room right before it happened," I said. "And we've heard how you feel about string players."

Harvey had a wild look in his eye. "I've seen you guys talking behind my back. I know you think I'm strange. Well, maybe I am. But I'm not crazy. Why would I ruin a two hundred and fifty thousand dollar instrument?"

"Who said it was worth two hundred and fifty thousand dollars?" I asked.

"Oh, I just heard it someplace."

"You seem to have a way with needle-nose pliers," said Splat. "Ever done any electrical wiring, Harv? Like in an automatic sprinkler system?"

Harvey stood up suddenly, strode across the room, and yanked open the door. "I think you'd better leave now."

"Do we have to?" asked Splat.

I took his elbow and guided him to the door. "You know what Emily Post says. Never argue with your host, especially if he's holding a knife."

We stopped at a McDonald's down the street to gather our wits and a couple of Big Macs. On the way back to the car, Splat spoke up.

"You know what strikes me about this whole thing?" he said. "There sure are a lot of jealous people hanging around the orchestra."

I nodded. "Harvey, Buffy, Arnie—all of them have motives for wrecking Kevin's violin. Then there's Myron, who just happens to be the most logical suspect of the bunch."

We climbed into the Packard. "These seats are a little lumpy," I said.

"That's impossible," said Splat. "They're stuffed with genuine duck down, just like you'll be if you don't stop bad-mouthing my Packard."

"I'm telling you, there's a big lump right here." I reached under me and felt around. My hand touched the corner of something hard. Resting on top of the seat was a cassette tape in a plastic box.

"Car's nice," I said, "but your housekeeping could use some work."

"Sizzle, that's not my tape. It wasn't here before."

I looked at the box. "It's the B Minor Mass, by Bach."
I opened it and a piece of paper fell to the floor. I picked
it up and unfolded it, revealing a four-line poem. Like
the one tied to the pigeon's leg, it was written in letters
cut out of a magazine.

> As you're playing this music
> Look out for the pun.
> You'll get a message
> Before it's all done.

> The Merry Prankster

"I thought the pigeons were supposed to be the last
prank," I said.

"He must have been kidding," said Splat. "Pranksters
do that, you know."

"What do you think this 'message' is?"

"Let's play the tape and find out. Maybe it's a clue."

"If you ask me," I said, "it's got an ominous sound to
it."

"Come on, Sizzle, how dangerous can a pun be? Are
you afraid we'll die laughing?"

I examined the tape, then handed it to Splat. "Okay,
put it on. But we listen from outside the car."

"Good idea. It may contain deadly nerve gas. Or
worse yet, Kryptonite."

"Just play it, wise guy."

Splat stuck the tape in the cassette player and opened
the car doors, then we backed off to listen. We let the
tape run for a good ten minutes before either of us
spoke.

"Hear anything?" I asked finally.

"Yeah, my stomach's making funny noises. Must have been the fries."

"Maybe we should get back in the car," I said. "I'm starting to feel a little silly."

"I don't see why," said Splat. "Every time I pass a McDonald's there's at least one group sitting in the parking lot listening to Bach's B Minor Mass."

We climbed back in and got on the freeway with the tape still playing.

"At least the guy could have sprung for a good quality cassette," said Splat. "This one has a buzz in the background."

"Are you sure that's on the tape? It almost sounds like the car."

"For your information, the Packard Custom Eight does not rattle, knock, ping, buzz, or make any other noises associated with more common forms of transportation."

"Then what's that sound?" I asked.

Just then we went over a bump. There was a clunk in the backseat, and a moment later there was no doubt about what the sound was.

Bees. Hundreds of them.

Splat took one hand off the wheel, frantically trying to brush the bees away, and the car drifted into the next lane. Horns honked and tires squealed as people swerved to avoid us.

"Keep steering!" I yelled.

I rolled down my window, but the bees weren't going anywhere. In fact, the rushing air just seemed to stir them up more. I felt the first stings on my face and arms as I climbed over the seat and cranked down a second window. By the time I lowered a third window, the place sounded like a kazoo convention, and my back and shoulders were on fire.

Splat, in the meantime, was trying to pull over. Steering with one hand and swiping at bees with the other, he lurched across two lanes of freeway traffic amid a chorus of protesting horns. We did a quick boogaloo with a '77 Mustang, skidded off the shoulder of the road, and careened down an offramp, still going forty.

"Slow down!" I cried.

"They're stinging my foot!" he yelled back. "I can't get to the brake!"

We hurtled toward the bottom of the ramp, where a row of cars waited at a stoplight. Just as we were right on top of them, Splat spun the steering wheel to the left, and the Packard skidded to a stop in a bank of ivy. We threw open the doors and flung ourselves to the ground. As we watched, the bees poured out and buzzed off in search of new victims.

A couple of hours later, we walked out of the emergency room at the UCLA Medical Center. Or rather, I walked and Splat hobbled, having been stung several times on the foot.

"What I don't understand is, how did they get inside my shoe?" he said. "I found three dead bees in there."

"Disgusting way to die," I said.

"Speaking of disgusting, did you know you have a bite right on the end of your nose? You look like Bozo the Clown."

"I wouldn't talk, Mr. Stein. Or shall I call you Frank?"

He gingerly touched his swollen eye and fat lip. "You know, given the fact that we were just talking to Harvey Bitner, I'd like to hear what he has to say about all this."

A few moments later I was in a phone booth, listening to Harvey's phone ring and watching Splat press his nose against the outside of the booth like a puppy in a pet store.

"Hello."

"Harvey, this is Sizzle."

"I'm telling you, I didn't do it."

"Didn't do what?"

There was a pause. "I didn't destroy Kevin's violin. Why else would you be calling?"

"The Bee Minor Mass, Harv. We watched out for the pun, just like the note said. Unfortunately we were looking in the wrong place."

"What are you talking about?"

"The jar in the backseat, Harv. The one with the lid balanced on top, so it fell off at the first big bump."

A strange sound came from the other end of the line, sort of a cross between a hyena and machine-gun fire. It was a few seconds before I figured out that Harvey was laughing.

"I get it," he said finally. "You're trying to drive me insane, aren't you?"

"Uh, no. Not at all. Say, Harv, I should probably be going."

"Wacko, crazy, cuckoo, daffy, cracked, Looney Tunes. Well, it's not going to work."

"I'm sure it won't. *Ciao*, big guy." I hung up the phone and stepped out of the booth.

"Well?" said Splat.

"I never thought of it before, but it's got to be tough blowing into that tiny little reed year after year. Must build up tremendous pressure inside your head."

I told him about the conversation as we headed for the parking lot. When we arrived, Splat checked out the condition of his Packard for the twenty-third time since our freeway mishap.

"You're lucky the car landed in a soft place," I said. "There's not a mark on it."

"Are you kidding?" he whined. "Look at these ivy stains."

As he tried to wipe them off, I checked the backseat for clues. Aside from a few dead bees, I didn't see a thing. Then a flash of bright color caught my eye. I pulled a red scarf out from under the seat.

"Maybe you were right about Buffy after all," I said, showing Splat what I'd found.

When he saw the scarf, he snatched it from my hand and stuffed it into his pocket. "That's not Buffy's," he murmured, turning away. "Come on, let's go."

I wasn't going to say anything. After all, what did I care how Arthur Pauling spent his spare time? But halfway home, my mouth rebelled. "Who owns the scarf?" it blurted.

"Never mind," Splat said, staring at the road.

That was fine with me, but my mouth wasn't buying it. "You had a date last Friday night, didn't you? And this is her scarf."

"No."

This time it wasn't just my mouth that spoke. It was my heart, lungs, liver, kidneys, and gallbladder. "We're friends, Splat. Stop lying to me."

"I'm not lying," he said softly. "You'll just have to trust me."

I was going to say more, but his tone of voice stopped me. There was something sincere and almost sad about it. As we rode home in silence, it occurred to me that I had another mystery on my hands. This one had nothing to do with pranks, and I would have to solve it on my own.

9

• • • • • • •

It was in Topanga Canyon, but it might as well have
been Transylvania.

I'd been told there was a house in back, but from the
front all you could see was a dense thicket that rose up
from the street and covered the property like a small hill.
Once or twice I'd peered through the branches and
glimpsed the corner of a chimney or the peak of a
weather-beaten gable, but that was the closest I'd ever
come to actually seeing the place. In front was an old
wooden mailbox overrun with spiderwebs. Next to that,
a gravel driveway disappeared among the branches and
brambles.

This was the residence of Arthur Hadley Reavis Pauling III. Like Splat himself, it was ramshackle on the outside, with an interior no civilized man had been known to enter. I had once pressed Splat about why he didn't let me go inside, and he finally admitted that it had to do with his mother, who was the only other person living there. From what I could gather, she was a very large woman with a drinking problem and a foghorn voice. She had embarrassed him a few times in front of friends, and he'd vowed never again to let anyone meet her.

Across the street were more bushes, and it was behind these that I sat in my dad's car, Che Guevara, inhaling a jumbo burrito from one of my favorite ethnic junk-food emporiums, Felipe's Fallen Arches. It had been exactly one week since my dad had seen Splat at Chez Pierre, and tonight I was on a stakeout to see if Friday night dates were a regular part of Splat's social calendar. If they weren't, I'd just pack up my things and head home with a light heart and a heavy stomach. If they were . . . well, I'd cross that moat when I came to it.

I finished the burrito and waited. An hour went by, and another. The sun had long since gone down, and the air was starting to get chilly. I would have turned on the heater, but Che Guevara didn't have one. (It also didn't have turn signals, sun visors, a radio, or a backseat. So what do you expect from a Third World car?)

In spite of the cold, though, I was starting to feel better. After all, the longer I waited, the less likely it was that Splat was going on a date tonight. I kept trying to picture him in a coat and tie, but I just couldn't do it. It was becoming apparent that my dad had gotten confused at Chez Pierre and had mistaken someone else for Splat.

Then I saw it. Two lights were moving among the

bushes in front of the Pauling house, like a couple of goblins on patrol. I hunched down in my seat and watched as they drew closer. There was a rustling of branches, and out of the darkness came the Packard. Inside, I could make out Splat's unmistakable silhouette. He was alone.

The headlights swept past me, and for once I was grateful not to be driving a shiny new car. Like all good guerrilla fighters, Che was camouflaged—in this case by a paint job that had started out red and after many losing battles had taken on the color and texture of year-old brownies. I waited for a few moments, then pulled out from behind the bushes and followed.

Using the Packard's oval-shaped taillights as a guide, I followed Splat along the winding canyon road. It twisted and turned, climbing all the while. Watching from a safe distance, I was struck once again by the stately elegance and sheer bulk of Splat's car, which seemed to float and bob like a fat lady wearing an evening gown and bustle. By comparison, Che staggered along the road like a tubercular wino.

As the road grew steeper, the staggering became more pronounced. On each hill Che would wheeze and slow down, and I'd lose sight of my quarry. As I hurried to catch up at the top of one grade, I drove past a little market and saw the Packard parked in front. I quickly pulled off the road next to a row of trees, where I could watch without being seen. A moment later Splat emerged from the market. He was wearing a coat and tie.

That's when I knew with bone-numbing certainty that Splat had lied to me. As the Packard drove past me once again, I gunned the engine angrily. It coughed and died.

"Che," I pleaded, "don't do this to me."

I turned the key and pumped the gas pedal. The engine cranked furiously but wouldn't turn over. I tried again and again, watching in frustration as the Packard's taillights disappeared around the bend.

Ten minutes later, by begging and coaxing and delivering a few well-placed kicks, I managed to get the engine started. Che limped to the canyon road's summit, then down the other side to Pacific Coast Highway, but there was no sign of Splat. Unwilling to give up, I lurched through Santa Monica and into Beverly Hills, where I checked the parking lot of Chez Pierre. The Packard wasn't there. I waited around for a while longer, but for all the good it did I might as well have been watching reruns of "I Love Lucy."

What do you do at eight o'clock in Beverly Hills, all riled up with no place to go? For me, the answer was simple. Eat.

Most people don't know it, but Beverly Hills has some of the finest junk-food stands in Southern California. I hit every one of them during the next hour, desperately trying to drown my sorrows in preservatives. When that didn't work, I still wasn't in the mood to go home, so I tried to think of people I could visit in the neighborhood. One name sprang to mind: Kevin Lim. I hadn't talked to Kevin since Wednesday, when his father had grounded him.

When I arrived at Kevin's place, I was greeted by a high-pitched screech coming from the back of the house. It was enough to set my teeth, gums, and dental retainer on edge. I rang the bell, and the noise abruptly stopped. A few moments later, Kevin Lim answered the door.

"Hi," he said. "I was just practicing."

"That was you?"

He ducked his head and fidgeted. "My father says the only way to play better is to practice the things you're worst at. I guess I must really be improving, huh?"

"I see you got your bandages off," I said. "Are your hands still bothering you?"

"They're a lot better, thanks. You want to come in? My mom made some cookies."

"Hey, great, I'm starved."

I followed Kevin inside, grateful he hadn't asked about my bee stings. Besides the issue of vanity, I didn't want him feeling guilty about our mishap, since in a way we were investigating on his behalf.

We went into the kitchen, where he poured me a soda and set out enough chocolate chip cookies to open a Mrs. Fields franchise. I took one bite and decided that this table was where I wanted to spend the rest of my life.

After my third cookie I came up for air. I noticed Kevin was grinning. "My father's a pretty good violinist," he said, "but most people say my mom's the real virtuoso in the family."

"Speaking of your dad, didn't I read that he's playing a concerto with the Philharmonic tonight?"

"That's where he and my mom are."

"Don't you usually go, too?" I asked.

"Yeah, but I just didn't feel like it tonight."

I studied his face. "You're mad at him, aren't you."

Kevin swirled the ice in his soda, took a sip, and

swirled it some more. "He's not the easiest person to get along with, you know."

I thought back to the way Bradford Lim had strutted onto the stage at his recital, and the way he'd held the charred Stradivarius in his lap the next day, ignoring his son's bandaged hands.

"He's never complimented me on my playing," said Kevin. "Not once, in ten years. It's like he expected me to pick up the violin when I was six years old and start playing a Schubert sonata just because I'm the son of the great Bradford Lim."

"If I become a famous trumpet player," I said, munching on another cookie, "I'm not going to teach my kids the trumpet. I'll have them play trombone, or maybe the triangle."

"I wish my instrument was the kazoo. Life would be a lot simpler."

With three more bites I sent another cookie tumbling toward my stomach, where it came to rest somewhere between the taco and the chili dog with onions.

"I guess I'm lucky," I said. "My dad's my biggest fan."

"He is?"

"Yeah, unless he's off on cloud nineteen someplace. He tends to daydream."

"How about your mom?"

"She's a big-city attorney," I said. "Unfortunately the big city's three thousand miles away."

"My mom's great. I think she gives me twice as much attention to try to make up for my father. Sometimes it's almost enough."

"I'm sure your dad tries," I said.

"I don't expect him to be my best buddy or anything. He doesn't have to play catch with me or give me a hug before I go to bed. I know he's not that kind of person. All I'd like is a little respect, maybe some trust."

"Like letting you use his Stradivarius?"

Kevin nodded. "Or his Mercedes, or the compact disc player, or anything else he thinks is important."

"It's funny when you think about it," I said. "If a person doesn't trust you, sometimes it says more about them than it does about you."

I was talking about Kevin's father, but I was thinking about myself. When I'd asked Splat about the girl at Chez Pierre, he had asked me to believe him. Now I'd spent half the night secretly following him because I didn't trust him.

"I'll tell you what it says about my father," said Kevin. "He's not interested in me or my mom. All he cares about are his things. And himself."

"Don't you think that's a little harsh?"

"I've lived with him sixteen years, Sizzle."

We moved into the den, where Kevin put on a recording of Itzhak Perlman playing the Brahms Violin Concerto.

"Hey, isn't that the piece your father's doing tonight?" I asked over the music.

"Yeah," said Kevin. "But Perlman plays it better."

As the opening chords sounded I thought about Splat. As far as I knew, he'd never lied to me about anything. Sure, there was some evidence against him this time, but none of it was what you'd call conclusive. Why was I so determined not to trust him?

It couldn't be jealousy. That would be like envying the

girl across the street for her big ears, or coveting your neighbor's cockroaches. I had to admit, though, there was something inside me that didn't like the idea of Splat going out with anyone else. If he asked me out I'd turn him down, of course. But at least I wanted first right of refusal.

Still, it was an issue of trust. Strange as he might be, Splat was my friend. There was probably a perfectly good explanation for what he'd been doing. He said he was telling the truth, and that was good enough for me.

As I reached this conclusion, I suddenly felt like a burden had been lifted from my shoulders. Now I could look in the mirror and know I was doing the right thing. I could be proud, because I'd acted like a mature, responsible individual. Plus, I wouldn't have to spend my Friday nights sitting in an unheated car.

When I got home that night, the first thing I did was call Splat. I wasn't checking on him, you understand. I was just trying to reestablish that all-important bond of communication and trust. To my amazement, he answered.

"Splat, is that you?"

"No, it's Santa Claus. Rudolph and I are in town for a reindeer convention."

"I just didn't know if you'd be home, that's all."

"Is there some reason I shouldn't be?"

"Huh? No, no reason in the world."

"Well?" he asked.

"Well, what?"

"Why did you call? Not that it hasn't been fun so far."

"Oh." My mind raced. It came to a screeching halt in

Encino, right next to a pink BMW. "I was just thinking, of all the suspects in our case, the only one we haven't talked to is Buffy Dupree. You want to go see her tomorrow?"

"Good idea. I've got a few questions I'd like to ask her."

"Such as?"

"Such as how someone growing up in California develops a Boston accent."

"You know, Splat, you may not be so dumb after all."

"Are you kidding? I'm brilliant, and if you've got two or three hours I'll tell you why."

"I'll pass, thanks."

"How about a quick twenty-minute summary?"

"See you tomorrow, Splat."

10

• • • • • • •

It seems that the people of Encino are always one step behind their Beverly Hills neighbors. Their houses aren't as lavish. Their Mercedeses aren't as long. Their furs aren't as thick, or their analysts as expensive. This troubles the people of Encino. To make up for it, they've tried to establish a clear edge in another category: obnoxious behavior. After much hard work, they appear to be winning.

Take Buffy Dupree, for example. Only seventeen years old, she had already shown great promise by developing an award-winning sneer and learning to hold her nose so high you could actually see right up her nostrils. As

Splat and I stood on her front doorstep that Saturday afternoon, it was a sight I wasn't looking forward to.

Buffy herself answered the door. As usual, she looked as if she'd stepped right off the pages of *Vogue*. It made me a little uncomfortable, since the only pages Splat and I belonged on were those of *Mad* magazine.

Buffy stared at Splat's T-shirt, which said *Etude, Brute*. Then she looked at us, the tip of her nose already starting to edge upward.

"Why, hello there," she said.

"What's happening?" said Splat.

"I beg your pardon?"

"If you've got a minute," I said, "we'd like to talk with you."

She shifted uncomfortably. "Could this wait? I'm in the middle of buffing my nails."

"Hence the name," said Splat.

"Just a few questions," I said. "It won't take long."

Buffy sighed. "All right. Just don't touch anything, okay?"

She led us down a carpeted hallway that was covered with a long plastic runner. As we walked past the living room, I noticed more plastic draped over the tables and chairs.

"Just had the place painted?" I asked.

"No, silly. Those are to keep things clean."

"Stop me if I'm way off base," said Splat, "but what if you actually wanted to use those chairs?"

I jabbed him with my elbow. "Don't mind Splat," I told Buffy. "He loves to kid around."

Amazingly, there were no drop cloths in the den. To

make up for it, the furniture itself was upholstered in plastic. Buffy perched on a vinyl easy chair, in front of which was a stack of polish, tweezers, clippers, and emery boards. She picked up a buffer and began shining her nails.

We stood awkwardly in the doorway for a moment, then Splat flopped down on the couch and put his feet up on a coffee table. Buffy shot him a look that could sterilize.

"Just checking to see if you were paying attention," said Splat, removing his feet from the table.

I decided to jump right in before Splat could perform any other tests, such as blowing his nose on the drapes.

"I guess you were pretty disappointed when Mr. Pirelli called off the rehearsals," I said. "Especially with you playing first violin and all."

"Not really," said Buffy, studying her cuticles a little too closely.

"You know," I said, "some people in the orchestra thought you should have been concertmaster in the first place."

She looked up at me, genuine anger on her face. "Every afternoon I go in my room, shut the door, and practice for three hours. I've done it on Christmas, New Year's, the Fourth of July, my birthday—every day for the past ten years. I've worked hard to get where I am. But I don't have a famous father, do I?"

"Are you saying the auditions were fixed?" asked Splat.

"According to what Giuseppe tells me, it's not impossible," Buffy replied.

"Giuseppe?" I said.

It was as if I'd asked who George Washington was. "Giuseppe Cantini," she said, "just happens to be the finest violin teacher in town, and one of the world's leading authorities on the Stradivarius."

Splat and I glanced at each other, and Buffy continued. "Giuseppe's had dealings with Bradford Lim. He says the man is ruthless."

"I noticed that myself," said Splat. "No ruth whatsoever."

"Maybe that's true," I said, "but why take it out on Kevin?"

She stopped mid buff, and her delicate face turned hard. "Are you accusing me of something?"

"My, aren't we sensitive," said Splat.

She set down the brush and faced us squarely. "Look, don't pussyfoot around with me. Everybody in the orchestra knows you two have been playing detective. For your information I had nothing to do with ruining that violin or hurting Kevin."

I turned to Splat. "Did I say anything about a violin?"

"Not that I remember. To tell you the truth, Buffy, we're more interested in your umbrella."

"Pardon me?"

"I'm the kind of guy who always forgets his umbrella," said Splat. "It always impresses me when somebody plans for things like overhead sprinklers and flocks of pigeons."

Buffy's voice turned as frosty as a beer mug. "I always carry an umbrella in my violin case. Those pranks were as big a surprise to me as they were to you. I thought they were terrible."

"I could see that," said Splat. "Whenever one of them hit, you were headed for the exit."

"I'd suggest you do the same," said Buffy, getting to her feet. "This conversation is over."

"What do you think?" asked Splat as we drove off a few moments later.

"I don't know about you, but I have a sudden, inexplicable urge to do some research on the Stradivarius."

"Funny you should mention that. I understand there's a world-famous authority living in Pasadena."

We stopped at a phone booth in front of a little market and looked up Cantini's number. Splat manned the receiver, while I munched on some Doritos and a Mars bar I'd bought inside.

"Mr. Cantini, this is Arthur 'Ace' Pauling," said Splat. "I'm doing an article for my school newspaper on Stradivarius violins, and everyone in town says you're the guy to talk to. I was just wondering, do you have a few minutes to speak to me and my assistant?"

"Assistant!" I said.

"No, sir, I'm at a public phone. You'll have to bear with me. There's a bag lady here who keeps asking for change."

"Bag lady!"

Splat called out, "Ma'am, please let go of my pants leg. Okay, okay, here's a quarter." He turned back to the receiver. "Sorry, sir, she's very persistent. A half hour? Sure, you got it." He hung up and stepped out of the booth.

"Since when do high-school newspaper reporters have assistants?" I said.

"I realize it's unusual. But then, I'm an unusual person."

"Funny, I never noticed."

We parked in front of Cantini's building and headed down the alley. Coming the other way was an identical pair of swarthy, broad-shouldered men with sunglasses. Each wore a suit with a dark shirt and white tie and was carrying a violin case.

After they had passed by, Splat looked at me. "Group lessons," he said.

He knocked on the door, and a moment later it opened a crack. Two eyes peered out over a security chain. "Yes?"

"Mr. Cantini," said Splat, "I'm Arthur 'Ace' Pauling, and this is Prudence Szyznowski."

"She is your assistant?" he asked, looking over at me.

"And a darned good one, too," said Splat.

My gaze bored into the back of his neck like an electric drill.

The chain rustled, and the door opened the rest of the way to reveal a small, thin man wearing a goatee and a frown. He led us into his studio, which turned out to be a large room with acoustical tile on the walls and ceiling. There were chairs and music stands on one side and a workbench on the other, with a sink and refrigerator nearby.

"Nice place," said Splat. "From the alley I wouldn't have guessed you had so much room."

"Mr. Pauling," said Cantini, speaking with a slight Italian accent, "you are holding something back from me, correct?"

"Huh? What makes you say that?"

"Why should a high-school newspaper write a story about the Stradivarius violin?" he asked. "It seems unusual to me."

"We have a very active music program at our school," said Splat. "The kids are really into it."

Cantini crossed his arms and stared at Splat. His eyes were an intense brown, almost black.

"Actually," I said, "we got the idea because of Bradford Lim's violin. His son Kevin goes to our school."

I was hoping Cantini wouldn't ask which school, because in point of fact I had no idea where Kevin went.

"Which school?" asked Cantini.

I took a shot in the dark. "Bel Air Prep."

"Isn't that an all-boys school?" asked Cantini.

"Not anymore," said Splat quickly. "Funny you should mention it, though. Prudence here is the first female assistant reporter in the history of the newspaper. Right, Pru?"

I bit my tongue and nodded. "I suppose you heard about Bradford Lim's violin?" I said.

"And why would I know about that?" asked Cantini.

"It's a Stradivarius. I just thought you might have heard."

There was another long pause. Cantini stroked his goatee thoughtfully. "Yes, I have. I just wanted to see if you were telling me the truth. I'm pleased to see that you are."

I felt a pang of guilt, then promptly brushed it aside. Cantini motioned for us to sit down.

"I once played Bradford Lim's Stradivarius," he said.

"That was before Lim owned it, of course." He began to pace restlessly up and down the floor, speaking as he did.

"You see, for all my life as a musician and teacher I have loved the violins of Stradivari. I studied them, read about them, went to concerts where they were played. And always I have had one great dream: to own a Stradivarius for myself. Then one day ten years ago, I read of an auction that would take place in London. They were selling one of the greatest of these violins. I decided this was my chance.

"Musicians were there from all over the world. Before the auction, each of us was given an opportunity to try out the instrument."

"That must have been a thrill," I said.

Cantini shot me a sly grin. "Oh, yes, but not in the way you think. Like spirited stallions, many of the Stradivarius violins—including Lim's—are difficult to tame. The first few times playing them, even the best violinist sounds terrible. It takes weeks to master them. So the truth, young lady, is that I sounded like a rank beginner that day. But I heard enough to know that this was a great instrument. From the first moment I touched her I was in love."

"Her?" asked Splat. "Was there a lady bidding, too?"

Cantini smiled sadly. "I am speaking of the instrument itself. A fine violin is like a woman, my friend, and I had found the love of my life. Her shape, her color, her voice—everything about her was perfect."

"Mmm, I know what you mean," said Splat. "I once fell in love with a baseball bat. Never got to first base with her, though."

"As I held this beautiful creature in my arms," said Cantini, "I knew I had made the right decision. I would gamble everything I owned to get her. Everything!

"The bidding opened at fifty thousand dollars and quickly climbed to sixty. With each bid I was saying good-bye to another possession—my house, my car, my studio, my violins. But still I kept bidding. Finally there was just one other person left."

"Bradford Lim," I said.

Cantini nodded. "I was pacing the room, just as I am doing now. But Lim, he sat there with a cold heart and a blank face, making each new bid with a casual flick of his hand. At one hundred fifty thousand dollars I could go no higher."

"I thought the violin was worth two fifty," said Splat.

"It is now," Cantini replied. "Or rather, it was." Cantini stopped and gazed off into the distance. "I still remember the expression on Lim's face when he realized I was quitting. He looked right at me, and his mask dropped away, revealing an evil grin. The man knew I was suffering inside, and he enjoyed every minute of it."

"It must be hard for you to go to L.A. Philharmonic concerts and see Lim play," I said.

"I've never been," said Cantini. "Not once."

"You must have felt awful when you heard about the accident," I said.

"I am desolate when any Stradivarius is lost," he said.

"Who was this guy Stradivari?" I asked.

"He lived in the Italian city of Cremona in the late seventeenth and early eighteenth centuries. He worked with his two sons, using techniques known only to them. When the sons died, Stradivari's secrets died with them."

"What makes his fiddles so special?" said Splat.

"Fiddles!" said Cantini. "I suppose you call the Mona Lisa 'that broad'?"

"Matter of fact, I do. She gets on my nerves with that silly grin of hers."

"To answer your question," Cantini said huffily, "no one is quite sure why the Stradivarius is so special. Some say the shape is what does it. Others say the wood, or the varnish. If you ask me, it is all those things, plus the one ingredient that is impossible to duplicate: the genius of Stradivari."

He stopped pacing. "Would you like to see what a Stradivarius looks like?"

"I thought you didn't own one," said Splat.

Without answering, Cantini wheeled and walked across the room. Splat and I exchanged puzzled glances, then followed him to a large antique cabinet in the corner. Cantini unlatched it and swung open the doors. On the top shelf was a collection of what looked like music boxes. On the shelf below them was a violin.

Cantini picked it up and turned it so we could look inside. "See that label?"

I squinted to read it. "It says *GC*."

"If this were a Stradivarius," he said, "you would see the letters *AS.*"

"So what does the *GC* stand for?" asked Splat.

"Giuseppe Cantini!" I said. "It's a reproduction."

He nodded, smiling proudly. "After losing out to Bradford Lim, I realized that many people who want a Stradivarius cannot afford one. So I decided to give them the next best thing: reasonably priced reproductions that are accurate down to the last detail."

"Wow," said Splat. "Genuine fakes."

"As you can see," said Cantini, "they look quite authentic, and their sound is lovely—though not, of course, as good as the real thing."

He tucked the instrument under his chin and played a series of arpeggios, then launched into a sonata. Perhaps five minutes later he put down the violin and looked over at us with a blank stare. For a moment I thought he was going to ask who we were, but then his eyes focused and he smiled slightly.

"What do you think?" he asked.

"It's wonderful," I said.

"You know, Miss Szyznowski, if an instrument is made with enough love and care, it begs to be played. All day while I am teaching my students, I hear this violin. In the morning it whispers. In the afternoon it begins to murmur. By evening it is crying out for me to pick it up and release the music locked inside. That is why I spend my nights in this studio, playing. It's not my idea; the violin tells me to do it."

"Do you make many of these?" I asked.

"Three or four a year. I sell them to my students and other musicians I know. Every instrument is a little better than the last, because with each one I learn something new. I know my violins will never match up to those of Maestro Stradivari, but I like to think he would be pleased."

"You said some of your students own them," said Splat. "Just out of curiosity, does that include Buffy Dupree?"

I knew it was a mistake as soon as he said it. I was just hoping it would slip by Cantini.

It didn't.

Cantini nodded, then caught himself. His eyes narrowed. "May I ask how you know Miss Dupree?"

As I watched Splat's face, I could see the wheels turning. Unfortunately the gears were stripped.

"And please," said Cantini, "don't tell me you go to school with her. She doesn't attend Bel Air Prep."

I sighed. "Neither do we. We're in the Pirelli Youth Orchestra."

"Why did you lie to me?"

"We're special investigators for the FBI," said Splat.

"Can it, Splat," I said.

Cantini strode across the room and opened the door. "I see I've been too generous with my time, and perhaps with my words, too."

"Look, Mr. Cantini," I said, "we really didn't—"

"Get out," he said.

"Nice going," I said to Splat outside.

"Hey, thanks to me we got a new lead. Buffy owns a reproduction Strad."

"Great. What does it mean?"

"I have no idea."

"I have one," I said. "Let's eat."

Splat glanced at his watch. "Oh, no, it's six o'clock." He hurried off toward the car.

"What about our new lead?" I said, following along behind.

"Tomorrow."

A less trusting person might have asked Splat where he was going in such a hurry. I, of course, was too proud for that sort of thing. I didn't say a word about it on the trip home, where I arrived with my pride intact and teeth marks all over my tongue. As I entered the apartment, my dad was just leaving.

"Hey, Sizzle. If you want some dinner there's *foie de veau sauté* in the fridge."

"Great, what is it?"

"Fried calf's liver."

"Do we have peanut butter and jelly?"

"You don't know what you're missing." He gave me a peck on the cheek. "I'll be at Deseret's place."

"The woman down the street with the beads and the tie-dye van?"

"Yeah, that's the one."

"Dad, what do you see in these earth-mother types? Besides the boobs, I mean."

"Hey, Deseret's very hip."

"Those, too."

"Sizzle, I *am* your father, you know."

"Sorry. I just wish you'd date a few women who were into something besides baking bread and taking in stray animals. For instance, what about a career woman?"

"I tried that. It ended in divorce."

"Oh. Right."

"Gotta go, hon. I'm walking, so you can use the car if you want." He kissed me again and shuffled off.

I went out on the balcony and watched him amble down the sidewalk, thinking what a kind, gentle man he was and hoping there was somebody out there besides me who knew it.

I had a light dinner of peanut butter and jelly sandwiches, nachos, fries, Milk Duds, and Rocky Road ice cream, then sat there staring into space, wondering what the heck I was going to do for the next five hours. I looked through my dad's record collection and put on some Miles Davis. After a while I switched to Art Tatum, then Billie Holiday, but somehow they all just made me sad. I went into my room and tried practicing but found that I had a bad case of peanut butter chops. Besides, who wants to practice on a Saturday night? I put down my trumpet and picked up a book my dad had been reading called *Ten Steps to Cosmic Consciousness*. I tripped on the first step and skinned my knee. Finally I sat down in front of the TV. I'd been there five minutes when I realized I'd forgotten to turn it on.

I spotted the car keys on the coffee table and decided to take Che Guevara for a spin. I grabbed a sweatshirt, left a note for my dad, and hopped in the car. My original plan was to head for Westwood, but the wheel kept pulling to the left, and before long I was surprised to find myself on Pacific Coast Highway, at the entrance to Topanga Canyon. I decided it couldn't hurt to drive through.

I hung a right and started up the winding road. Che's engine rattled and thumped, showing all the compression of a butter churn. Luckily there wasn't much traffic, so my twenty-mile-an-hour pace didn't seem to bother anybody. I finally reached the top and started down the other side. Picking up speed, I rolled down the window and shivered excitedly as the cold wind whipped through the car. I rumbled down a straightaway and around a corner. Coming out of the turn, I approached the market where Splat had stopped the night before.

The Packard was parked in front.

Obviously it was a test. Fate had provided me with the perfect opportunity to show what a magnanimous, trusting person I'd become. All I had to do was keep driving. And that's just what I did. I whizzed by, exhilarated by my newfound maturity and self-control. Just then Splat walked out of the market, wearing a coat and tie.

Somewhere deep within the recesses of my brain there was a skirmish between the well-disciplined forces of maturity and a mob of bickering, leering dolts. The dolts won. By the time the dust cleared, Che had negotiated a hasty U-turn and was idling fitfully by the side of the road.

I squinted to find out who was in the car with Splat and didn't see anyone. A moment later the Packard pulled out of the parking lot. Careful not to kill the engine, I edged into the road and followed Splat at a safe distance. He was headed back through the canyon, in the direction I'd come from.

I managed to stay with him to the crest of the hill, and after that it was no trouble at all. If there was one thing Che could do, it was coast.

We emerged from the canyon and drove down Pacific Coast Highway, through West L.A., and into Beverly Hills. Somewhere up ahead, I thought, lived an orthodontist or tax attorney so wrapped up in his practice he'd failed to notice that his daughter was dating the Creature from the Black Lagoon.

Imagine my surprise when a short time later I looked up and saw the sign for Chez Pierre. There was a line of Mercedeses, Jaguars, and Ferraris in front waiting for valet parking. Splat pulled in behind.

What had happened to the orthodontist's daughter?

Was Splat going to meet her at the front door? If he was dining by himself, why not go to McDonald's the way any self-respecting teenager would?

I parked Che on a side street and hurried around to the front of the restaurant. I was in luck. There was a canopy leading from the door to the curb, and on either side of it was an expanse of immaculately trimmed hedge. By slipping in behind the shrubbery at the edge of the building I could make my way to within a few feet of the entrance without being seen. I peered around the hedge and found myself looking over the shoulder of a uniformed doorman. On the sidewalk, parking attendants buzzed around the cars like flies on a box of jelly donuts. Just as I was getting my bearings, the Packard reached the front of the line.

Something strange was going on. The first thing I noticed was that one of the attendants opened the door on the passenger's side, which was unoccupied. Okay, fine. He wants to check out the interior of a classic automobile, or maybe get a little cross ventilation going. But wait. He seems to be smiling and talking to the front seat, though I can't be sure because of my angle of vision. Could it be that the guy has burned rubber on one too many Cadillacs? Is his steering wheel a little loose? A moment later I had my answers. And a whole new set of questions.

Out of the car stepped a miniature girl. I hadn't seen her in the car because she was no more than four feet tall. But she was perfectly proportioned, and she was beautiful. Her hair was blonde. Her cheeks, as smooth and rounded as a porcelain vase, were the color of roses.

She had a cute little upturned nose, and blue eyes that would make Barbie jealous.

The girl took Splat's arm and, smiling shyly at the attendant, made her way toward the entrance, where I watched from behind a bush. As they approached the door, I grabbed hold of a branch and leaned forward to get a better view. I suppose I was hoping to spot some clue to her identity, or a flaw in that perfect complexion, or maybe a wind-up key in her back. With the first glance I knew a couple of things for sure: One, she was just as beautiful as I had thought; and two, the branch had broken, and I was going to fall flat on my face.

When you're five feet eleven, you can't just slip to the ground, then quickly pop back up with a giggle and a grin. It's more involved than that, like the descent of a giant redwood, or the mating dance of a giraffe. You feel yourself going, so you pinwheel your arms and swivel your head and try to get a foothold with your size twelves. Of course it never works, because in addition to being tall you're also a klutz. So you fall in a heap, then look up and try to say something clever.

"Pardon me, I'm with Cal Tech," I said. "We're running some seismic experiments." I turned toward the bushes and called out, "Did that one register, Jerry?"

"Hello," said Splat.

"Six point five? Okay, let's call it a day, huh?"

"You followed me," said Splat. His expression fell somewhere between tired and angry. I wasn't sure of his date's response because she had ducked for cover behind Splat, like a frightened rabbit darting behind a tree.

"You lied," I said.

"You don't understand," he said.

"You didn't introduce us," I said.

Splat looked at his friend, then put an arm around her protectively. "Sorry, Sizzle, but we have to go inside."

The girl hesitated. In a voice as tiny as the rest of her she asked, "You're Sizzle?"

"As far as I can tell, yes."

"I've heard a lot about you," she said.

"You have?"

She hesitated, then said, "You wouldn't want to join us for dinner, would you?"

Splat's jaw dropped to his chest with a dull thud.

I was wearing jeans, sneakers, and a sweatshirt, which at Chez Pierre wasn't exactly the uniform of the day. And with a depth charge of peanut butter and nachos still on its way to the bottom of my stomach, you couldn't say I was starving. But there was something at work here that was far stronger than either embarrassment or hunger. It was curiosity. I walked through the door.

When the maitre d' saw me, his eyebrows executed a launch that would have made NASA proud. He sidled over and began Snooty Restaurant Speech Number 3, the one that includes words such as *attire* and *clientele*. Then he looked over my shoulder and saw Splat's date, and his expression changed.

"Madame," he purred to her, "how are we this evening?"

"We're fine," I said. "How about hustling up a table for three."

The maitre d' shot her a "say it ain't so, Joe" look. She nodded. He sighed.

"Follow me, please."

I figured we'd be stuck off in a corner somewhere between the dumpster and the employees' shower, but to my surprise we were led to an elegant table in a private room.

"Hey, thanks," I told the maitre d' as we sat down. "This is swell."

"Young lady," he replied, "everything we do here is swell." He did an about-face and minced off.

There was a long silence. "Well," I said finally, "am I going to find out what's going on, or shall we just study the silverware pattern?"

Splat shifted in his chair, trying without success to find a comfortable position.

"How often do you come here?" I asked.

"Not that often," said Splat.

His date blinked rapidly a few times and cleared her throat. "Arthur and I come here every week, sometimes on Friday and sometimes on Saturday."

Once again Splat looked up at her in surprise. Suddenly I felt as if I was part of a play in which everybody but me had a script. I didn't like the feeling.

"You know," I told her, "Arthur's friends call him Splat. There's kind of an interesting story behind it. See, when he was a kid he used to go to the marsh behind his house and catch frogs—big, fat ones. Then he'd carry them out to the street and throw them in the air as high as he could. Funny how nicknames get started, isn't it?"

To my amazement, she smiled. Then she started to giggle. Before I knew it, her tiny shoulders were shaking with laughter.

"You think that's funny?" I asked. "Wait'll you hear what he did with snails and a salt shaker."

Still giggling, she shook her head. "He's really not like that, you know."

"Tell that to the snails," I said.

"Maybe we should order," said Splat.

"How about an appetizer of chilled facts on the half shell," I told him. "For my entree I'd like the truth, plain and simple. If you can't give me that, I'll take your head on a platter."

"Arthur," said the girl, "let's tell her."

What was I about to find out? That they were a runaway carnival act? That Splat was secretly a restaurant critic for the *New York Times*? That he was a Russian spy, and the girl was his contact? My mind raced, like a dragster without a steering wheel.

"I already told her," said Splat.

"Huh?" I said. "Did I nod off for a second?"

"Sizzle, when you asked me about Chez Pierre in the car that day, do you remember what I said?"

"Yeah, you said my dad must have seen someone else."

"No, after that."

I thought back. "You made up some excuse. Something about spending a quiet evening at home."

Splat shook his head. "No. I said I spent a quiet evening with my mother."

He gazed at me without speaking. His date did the same. After a moment she extended her hand and said in a shaky voice, "Sizzle, I'm Gwendolyn Pauling."

12

• • • • • • •

"I get it," I said. "If I shake your hand, a couple of guys in white coats step out from behind a curtain and drag me off."

"I know it's hard to believe," she said. "I guess I don't look much like a mother."

"Look, I don't want to seem rude, but I know for a fact that Splat's mother is overweight and alcoholic," I said.

"That was just a cover story," said Splat. "I pretended to be embarrassed about it so you wouldn't come in the house. Actually, my mother's just very shy."

I studied his companion. Then I reached out and took her hand. Instead of shaking it, I examined it carefully. It was soft, but it wasn't smooth. There were wrinkles in the palm and around the knuckles.

"Mind if I ask how old you are?" I said.

"Thirty-seven," she replied softly.

"If you're his mother, how come you're so . . . and he's so . . ."

"I resent that," said Splat.

"Arthur takes after his father," she explained.

"Hey," said Splat.

She patted his hand. "Now dear, you know what I mean."

"I feel like an idiot," I said.

"It's all right," she said. "I know I don't look my age."

"No, I mean the way I've been following Splat around. I was convinced he was dating some orthodontist's daughter from Beverly Hills."

"You were?" said Splat.

"Not that it mattered, of course," I said. "I was just upset because I didn't think you were telling me the truth."

"I see," he said.

"No, what I mean is, I think trust is very important in a relationship. I mean, in a friendship. You know what I mean."

"Absolutely," Splat said.

I turned to his mother. "So you're Mrs. Pauling. Wow."

"Please, call me Gwendolyn."

Gwendolyn. Somehow it fit. "Gwendolyn, it looks like you're a regular here. If you're so shy, doesn't it bother you to be out in public?"

"Food is one of the few ways I indulge myself. On Friday and Saturday nights Arthur drives me to a fine restaurant. It's the only time I go outside."

"Must be tough, staying in the house all the time."

She gave me a sad little smile. "It's a life I'm used to. Between catalogs and Arthur's Delivery Service I manage quite nicely."

"Arthur's Delivery Service?"

"You hire the best, we do the rest," said Splat.

"Why did you invite me in?" I asked her.

"I couldn't resist the chance to meet you, Sizzle. Arthur's told me so much about you."

"Height, weight, stuff like that," said Splat.

"He says you're really quite wonderful," she said.

"Wonderful penmanship," Splat added quickly. "Neat, easy to read, just great."

That's when the waiter arrived. It was just as well, since I wasn't in the mood to demonstrate my handwriting. We ordered, then Gwendolyn began asking me questions about myself. It's a subject I like talking about, and she didn't seem to mind listening. As we ate, she grew more and more relaxed. By the end of the meal, she was chatting comfortably. When the waiter brought the check, she slid it toward her and opened her purse.

"I'll pay for my part," I told her.

"Don't be silly."

"It's no problem," I said. "I don't want to mess up your food budget."

"My dear," she said, "Arthur and I could eat here every night of the week and not mess up our food budget."

As I considered this startling bit of information, she paid the check and turned to me. "So, what did you think of Chez Pierre?"

"Delicious. Almost as good as a little place I like in Mar Vista."

"I'd love to try it," she said. "Isn't that near where you live?"

"It *is* where I live. My dad could show Pierre some things that would curl his Cuisinart. Maybe sometime you and Splat could come over and see for yourselves. How about, say, Monday night?"

She swallowed hard and looked down at the table.

"That's really nice of you," said Splat, "but we've sort of got our regular places."

Gwendolyn Pauling slowly brought her eyes back up, took a deep breath, and said, "Thank you, Sizzle. We'd love to."

"Great!"

"But on one condition," she said.

"What's that?"

"That you join us for dessert at our house tonight."

Half an hour later I was eating apple pie inside Fort Pauling, which turned out to be as neat and tidy on the inside as it was overgrown on the outside.

Gwendolyn sat across from me in a special high-legged chair, sipping tea. She seemed nervous but excited. "It seems strange having someone else in the house."

"You sure you're okay, Mom?" asked Splat. He placed a hand on her arm, and she nodded.

"This pie is incredible," I said.

Gwendolyn blushed. "An old Boston recipe. Arthur's grandmother used to make it."

"We lived with her and my grandfather when I was growing up," said Splat.

"Let me guess," I said. "Their house had a marsh behind it where lots of frogs lived."

His mother smiled. "We had some wonderful times there, even if the frogs didn't."

Splat cocked his head to one side and looked at me. "Do you hear something?"

I listened for a moment. "Music. The *William Tell* Overture. Hey, your neighbors have good taste."

"Our neighbors are out of town."

"Then the neighbors' burglars have good taste."

As Splat got up to check, there was a loud *thwang,* and an arrow sprouted in the wall behind him.

In two quick steps he was at his mother's side, pulling her from her chair and diving beneath the table, where he covered her body with his. Always quick to recognize a good idea, I joined them. As we huddled there, we heard the strains of the famous *William Tell* fanfare, better known as the Lone Ranger's theme.

"I can't believe Tonto would do this," I said.

"Remember the story of William Tell?" said Splat. "He shot an apple off his son's head with a bow and arrow."

"The Merry Prankster?" I said.

"No, William Tell."

"Who's the Merry Prankster?" asked Gwendolyn.

"I'll tell you later, Mom," said Splat.

In a few minutes the overture had ended, with no sign of any more arrows. Splat got a couple of flashlights, and we crept to the window and peered out. No one was there. We went outside, split up, and searched the yard.

A moment later Splat called me over. Nestled in the grass by his feet was an inexpensive cassette player.

He picked it up and pushed the eject button. Out popped a tape labeled *Rossini's Greatest Hits*, along with a folded sheet of paper. I opened it and saw a message, once again written in letters cut out of a magazine.

> You're asking for trouble;
> That's plain to see.
> This "hit" was a miss,
> But the next one won't be.

> ### The Merry Prankster

"This is great!" said Splat as we headed back inside. "It means we're on the right track."

"It means we may die," I said.

"Die?" said Gwendolyn, who met us at the door. "Arthur, what's going on?"

"Sizzle and I have been doing a little investigating," said Splat. "I would have told you, but I didn't want you worrying."

"I'm supposed to worry," she said. "I'm your mother. Now will you please explain what's going on?"

We sat down at the table, and Splat outlined the events of the past week. When he finished, she said, "Arthur, I'd like you to go to the police."

"We already went. They just laughed."

"Someone shot an arrow into our house," she said with surprising firmness. "If you don't go to the police, I will."

"She's right," I said. "We should tell Denton what's been happening."

110

"Sizzle, we're about to solve the case."

"We are?"

"Think about it," he said. "The prankster tried to scare us off once with the bees. So why would he try to scare us again unless we were getting warmer?"

"There's a certain logic to that," I admitted.

"And what are the only leads we've followed up since that first warning?"

I thought back for a minute. "Buffy," I said finally. "And Cantini."

"Right. They both must have destroyed the violin for revenge—Buffy against Kevin, and Cantini against Kevin's father." Splat grinned. "You know, sometimes my brilliance overwhelms me."

"Just one problem," I said. "After talking to Cantini, I guarantee he'd never destroy a Strad. Especially that one."

"Hmm. Okay, then maybe Buffy handled the whole thing by herself, pranks and all."

"Not the Buffy I know. The only bow she'd go near is the kind you use on a fiddle."

Splat looked like a kid whose balloon had just popped. "Geez, and I thought I had it all figured out."

"How can you be so sure this Mr. Cantini wouldn't destroy a Stradivarius?" asked Gwendolyn.

"He talks about them like they're alive or something," Splat said. "He even makes his own reproductions of them."

"Oh, my God," I said.

"Are you all right, dear?" asked Gwendolyn.

"Oh, my God."

"I didn't mention it," said Splat, "but Sizzle's a very religious person."

111

I got up and started pacing back and forth.

"She's also big on exercise," he said.

"It all fits together," I said.

"Religion and exercise?"

"Cantini *is* involved. It explains everything."

"Then why am I confused?" said Splat.

"Did you notice how upset he was when he found out we were in the orchestra? If he'd known, he never would have talked about Bradford Lim's violin. Because that's the key to the whole thing."

"I'm sorry, dear," said Gwendolyn, "but you've lost us."

I stopped pacing and sat back down. "Everything Cantini told us was true except for one thing: He never gave up the idea of getting that Stradivarius."

"So why would he destroy it?" asked Splat.

"He didn't."

"Sizzle, we were there. We saw the violin burn, and we saw the ashes afterward." He turned to his mother and shook his head sadly. "I knew it would happen eventually. All those preservatives have pickled her brain."

"Splat, I'm not denying we saw a violin destroyed. All I'm saying is that it wasn't the Strad."

"But it looked just like—" He stopped abruptly in the middle of his sentence. "Oh, my God."

"We've got a convert," I said.

"I don't understand," said Gwendolyn.

"It was one of Cantini's reproductions," Splat said. "Buffy must have switched them."

"They planned the whole thing from the beginning," I said. "Buffy found out what music we'd be playing, and she and Cantini set up some pranks, knowing everyone would blame Myron. The firecracker prank looked like one in a series, but in fact it was the reason for all the pranks in the first place."

"When Kevin walked up to the podium after the rehearsal that day," said Splat, "Buffy switched violins, lit the firecrackers, and made a beeline for the door, carrying the real Strad. She knew that by the time the reproduction stopped burning, no one would be able to tell it from the original."

"So Cantini got his Strad and Buffy got her revenge," I said. "Ingenious."

Splat turned to Gwendolyn. "Mother, you may congratulate us."

"Congratulations, dear."

Splat beamed. "I love spontaneous praise."

"If you don't mind, I have a question," said Gwendolyn.

"Sure," he said. "In a complex case like this, only the most brilliant investigative minds can grasp everything the first time."

"Didn't you tell me Kevin Lim borrowed his father's violin on impulse?" she asked.

"That's right."

"Then how could Buffy and Mr. Cantini plan everything in advance?"

"Are you kidding?" said Splat. "The answer's very simple. Extremely simple answer. Sizzle, you want to help me out on this?"

"Sure," I said. "The answer is that we have no idea."

"See?" Splat said to his mom. Then he turned to me. "We don't?"

"She's right, Splat," I said. "Our theory's got a hole in

it big enough to drive your Packard through. Buffy couldn't have known until that morning that Kevin had the Strad. We're back to square one."

Splat sighed. "Couldn't we at least say square two?"

"Okay, if it makes you feel better."

Gwendolyn took a sip of tea from her porcelain cup, then carefully replaced it on the saucer. "Buffy didn't get involved because of the Stradivarius, did she?"

I shook my head. "Her motive was revenge."

"Then couldn't she still have planned the pranks?"

"You know," said Splat, "she may be right."

He gazed down at the table for a few moments, then looked back up. "Okay, try this on for size. Buffy sets everything up, just like we said, only she's on her own. Her goal is to get back at Kevin by wrecking his violin. But when she goes to light the firecrackers, she notices the Strad. She'd recognize it, of course, being a student of Cantini. She doesn't want to destroy it, but she also doesn't want to abort her plan. So she does some quick thinking and replaces the Strad with her own violin."

"Which was a reproduction!" I said.

"Right. She puts the Strad in her own case, lights the firecrackers, and leaves."

"And probably drives straight to Cantini's place to show off her prize. So Cantini wasn't involved at the beginning, but now he's in it up to his Adam's apple."

"Not to mention William Tell's apple," said Splat. "I'll bet if we checked, we'd find a bow and arrow hidden in one of his closets."

"There's just one thing," I said. "If Cantini didn't help Buffy with the first few pranks, who did?"

"It could have been anybody—Harvey, Arnie, her

brother, a girlfriend. In fact, those early pranks might actually have been Myron. Buffy would have seen those pranks, giving her the idea for the firecrackers."

Gwendolyn patted Splat's shoulder. "That's very good, dear. I'm sure the police will be interested to hear this."

"But it's just a theory," said Splat. "We can't go to the police until we get some evidence."

"Such as a hole in your skull?" I said. "Forget it, Splat. We're going to see Denton first thing tomorrow morning. Besides, he has all the evidence we need."

"He does?"

"I'll explain later," I said. "But don't feel bad, Splat. Only the most brilliant investigative minds can grasp everything the first time."

13

· · · · · · ·

Detective Niles Denton walked into the lobby of the police station with a Sunday paper under his arm, carrying a danish and a cup of coffee. He looked at Splat's T-shirt.

"*The Ives have it,*" he said. "What's that supposed to mean?"

"Ever heard of Charles Ives?" asked Splat.

"Didn't he play third base for the Mets?"

"Yeah, that's the guy," said Splat. "You're sharp, Niles."

It was eight o'clock in the morning. I'd called Denton a half hour earlier and told him that if he'd meet us at the station, we'd show him new evidence in the Lim case.

Denton unlocked his office, tossed the paper onto his desk, and flopped down into his chair. "Okay, what have you got?"

"We don't have it," I said. "You do."

"Come again?"

"The evidence in the Lim case," I said, "is in the Lim case."

"Look, Szyznowski, I didn't drag myself out of bed to play games."

"You're no fun anymore," said Splat.

"I'm talking about Bradford Lim's violin case," I said. "You're keeping it here at the station, right?"

Without answering, Denton went over to a metal cabinet and carefully removed the violin case. He opened it, revealing the same charred remains we'd seen before.

"Great evidence," he said.

"Got a flashlight?" I asked.

"For what?"

"She wants to check my tonsils," Splat said.

Denton shook his head. "How did I ever get involved with you people?"

"Are we involved?" said Splat.

Muttering to himself, Denton rummaged around in a drawer and handed me a flashlight. I shone it into the violin, searching what was left of the inside surfaces. After a few minutes I switched off the flashlight and handed it back to Denton.

"Oh, well," I said. "It was a good idea."

"What were you looking for?" asked Denton.

"A label showing whether this was a real Stradivarius. Unfortunately, it was burned along with the rest of the violin."

He leaned back in his chair and squinted through the cigarette smoke. "Does this mean I'm going to have to listen to some screwball theory of yours?"

"Not unless you want to hear about a quarter of a million dollars in stolen property and two murder attempts," said Splat.

Denton groaned. "You guys give cockamamy a bad name."

"I guess we could always go to one of the other detectives," I said.

"Okay, okay. Let's hear it." He slumped down in his chair, took a long drag on his cigarette, and nodded for me to begin.

I outlined our case against Buffy and Cantini, describing means, motive, and opportunity. When I finished, he shook his head. "Pretty farfetched."

"Maybe so," said Splat, "but we know we're right. Cantini told us."

"Huh?" said Denton.

"In deeds, not words."

I related the incident involving the bees, and Denton sat up a little straighter. The interview with Cantini brought him up a few inches more. By the time I mentioned the arrow, he looked like the poster boy for National Posture Week.

"So how do you like our cockamamy theory?" said Splat.

"I've got to think about it. But in the meantime I don't want you two messing with this thing anymore. It's too dangerous."

"What are you going to do?" I asked him.

"My job."

"If I were you, I'd get a search warrant for Cantini's studio," said Splat.

"If you were me," said Denton, "the police department would be in big trouble."

We rolled up to my apartment a few minutes later, and I invited Splat in for a quick snack. As we reached the top of the stairs, I fumbled in my pocket for the key and almost tripped over something. In front of the door was a handsome wooden object about the size of a shoe box.

"Nice doorstop you got there," said Splat.

I picked it up and examined it. The top was covered with hand-carved designs. On the back were a pair of brass hinges, and on the front was a latch.

"This looks familiar," I said.

"Cantini's place!" said Splat. "It's a music box, like some of the ones he had in that cabinet with the violin."

"Are you thinking what I'm thinking?" I said.

"No, I'm thinking what I'm thinking. But I think I know what you think I'm thinking."

"What do you think I'm thinking?"

"I think you think I'm thinking we shouldn't open that box."

"That's exactly what I was thinking," I said. "What do you think?"

"I think we'd better stop this or I'm going to run down the stairs screaming."

"Splat, there could be anything inside."

"That's not true. There couldn't be a Ping Pong table. There couldn't be a Buick."

"There could be a bomb," I said.

"Yeah, there's that."

We stood there, staring at the box.

"Come on," I said, carefully picking it up. I went inside and got a spool of twine, then descended the stairs and headed for the empty parking lot next door.

Splat hopped nervously alongside. "What are you doing?"

"Getting ready for the senior prom."

I strode across the asphalt and set the box down in front of a concrete light pole. I squatted and unlatched the box lid without opening it. Unspooling the twine, I tied one end to the latch and looped the rest around the pole. Then, holding the spool, I backed up in the direction I'd come from, letting the twine play out as I went. When I reached the end of the spool I was fifty yards away, behind a corner of the garage. Splat crouched next to me.

"Do we really want to do this?" he said.

"Splat, there's no one around. The worst that could happen is the asphalt gets rearranged."

I began to pull. The line tightened until it stretched from my hand to the pole without touching the ground. I looked over at Splat. One more tug would raise the lid.

I tugged.

There was no explosion. There was no bomb. There was no flash or crash or bang. What there was, was music. It floated across the parking lot, played in those tinkly bell-like sounds you hear in music boxes.

"Sounds like Haydn," I said.

"Yup. Symphony Number 101."

We looked at each other and said in perfect unison, "The *Surprise Symphony*."

"The question is," I said, "what's the surprise if it's not a bomb?"

"Black widows? A Hostess Twinkie?"

"Maybe the surprise is that there is no surprise," I said. "He could just be thumbing his nose at us."

"On the other hand, it could be a delayed explosion."

"It would have blown by now. I'm going to look." I started toward the music box.

"Sure you don't want to reconsider?" he asked. I kept walking. He called after me, "It's been great knowing you."

I reached the music box and peered inside. It was empty, except for a folded sheet of paper. As I bent down to get it, Splat yelled, "Don't, you might trigger the firing mechanism!"

I picked up the paper and unfolded it. There was another message, made up of letters cut out of a magazine.

> In Memorial Park
> There's a hole by the walk.
> Be there at seven
> If you want to talk.
> You'll learn about Strads;
> There's a lot you should know.
> But if you tell Denton,
> This Prankster won't show.
>
> M. P.

As I read the message, Splat appeared at my elbow. "I couldn't stand by and see you blown to bits," he said.

"Thanks. You would have been just in time to sweep up the pieces."

He skimmed the note and gave a low whistle. "Wow, a chance to meet the Merry Prankster himself."

"Or herself, or themselves."

"Shall we rent a hall?"

"You know what bothers me?" I said.

"Indigestion? Athlete's foot?"

"The prankster knows too much about us," I said. "He knew we were at your house last night, even though I'd never been there before. He knows we've been talking to Denton. He could be watching us right now."

We glanced around uneasily. There was a rustling in a bush nearby, and a squirrel scampered across the corner of the parking lot. We jumped, then looked at each other and started to laugh. Somehow it sounded hollow.

"You think we should go to the park tonight?" Splat said in the awkward silence that followed.

"No," I said. "But that never stopped us before."

14
· · · · · · ·

It had started out as Glazer Park, but after World War II somebody in the city planning department had the bright idea of putting statues and war memorabilia there and changing the name to Memorial Park. It was a great place for birds to practice their marksmanship, and a good spot for a picnic if you didn't mind George Patton or Ulysses S. Grant looking over your shoulder. I'd always thought the name change made the place sound more like a cemetery than a park, but as Splat and I got out of the car a few minutes before seven, that was something I didn't want to dwell on.

I shone a flashlight on the note. " 'A hole by the walk.' What do you think that means?"

"I don't know. A golf hole? A ditch? A loaf of bread?"

"Pardon me?"

"Hole wheat."

"Go to your room," I said. "On second thought, stick around. This place gives me the willies."

A paved walkway led into the park, curving among the trees and picnic tables. We followed it, going slowly and keeping our eyes peeled for holes of any size or shape. A few lights were scattered through the park, but most of them weren't working. An owl hooted softly. Crickets scratched out a steady pulse. There was a rustling off to the left, and we froze.

"Must have been the wind," said Splat after a few moments. We moved forward again, our nerves stretched as tight as a pair of bongo drums. A moment later Splat stopped abruptly.

"There," he breathed, pointing to a spot next to the walkway. It was a hole the size of a basketball, dug on a slant to a depth of perhaps a foot.

I looked around, puzzled. "What's it doing here?"

"Maybe the prankster dug it as a marker so we'd know where to meet."

"If he needed a meeting place, what's wrong with Robert E. Lee or General Custer?" I asked, gesturing at the nearby statues.

"Who cares?" said Splat. "The big question is, who's going to step out from behind those trees? Buffy? Cantini? Harvey Bitner? Arnie Klingmeyer? Myron Mann? And what are they going to tell us?"

I shifted nervously from foot to foot, scanning the area for signs of the Merry Prankster. My watch showed 6:57, then 6:58. At 6:59, I started silently counting down the seconds.

At precisely seven o'clock, music began to play.

"Sounds like our friend," said Splat.

"Hello?" I called out.

There was no answer. There was only the music, slow and stately, measured and graceful, winding its way among the branches.

"Boy, that piece sounds familiar," said Splat. "What's the name of it?"

I'd heard it a hundred times, but for some reason I couldn't think of the title. "Just give me a second. It's right on the tip of my tongue."

"Here, open your mouth and I'll look."

"It's that guy with the funny name. Starts with a *P.*"

"Puccini, Poulenc, Paganini, Paderewski . . ."

"No, none of those guys."

"Prokofiev, Purcell, Perry Como, the Platters . . ."

"Splat, you're not helping."

The music was getting louder and louder, as though someone was gradually turning up the volume. The tone became distorted, and before long the lilting melody was blasting away with all the subtlety of a jackhammer. Just when I thought I couldn't stand it anymore, an unseen hand flipped a switch, and the music stopped mid phrase. The echo died out, leaving only the birds and the crickets.

"Pachelbel!" I exclaimed.

"Oh, no!" said Splat.

An explosion ripped through the night. Splat threw himself against me, and we tumbled to the ground. A few feet away, there was a loud thud.

"You okay?" Splat asked breathlessly.

"Yeah."

He scrambled to his feet and raced toward the trees, with me close behind. We heard the slam of a car door and the squeal of tires. Through the trees we saw two red taillights disappearing into the distance.

Splat shook his head in disgust. "We might have caught him if I'd just figured it out a few seconds earlier."

"Figured what out?"

He led me back to the walkway. Right where we'd been standing was a second hole just like the first. At the bottom was what looked like an old bowling ball.

"The name of that piece was Pachelbel's *Canon,*" he said. "Which would make this Pachelbel's cannonball."

"Killer pun," I said.

We walked over in the direction of the explosion. In a clearing not far away was a Civil War cannon.

"Now we know why he chose Memorial Park," I said. "It was the only place in town with the equipment he needed."

"And it explains why he wanted us by that hole. He must have taken a practice shot to see where the cannonball would land."

"You'd think they would disarm this thing," I said, running my hand along the top of it.

"They did," Splat said, examining the relic with his flashlight. "But the prankster drilled a hole in the back of the barrel and ran a fuse inside. All he needed then was some gunpowder and a cannonball. Crude but effective."

"I might say the same thing about you."

"Was that a compliment?"

"Definitely. Thanks for tackling me back there."

Splat grinned. "Anytime."

We headed back to the car. "I guess we should tell Denton about this," I said.

"I was just thinking the same thing. He's going to be mad we didn't come to him with the note."

We went straight to the police station and were told Denton would be back shortly. About eight o'clock he stormed through the door.

"Could we talk to you for a minute?" I asked.

"No," he said, walking right by. He went into his office and slammed the door.

"Do you think he already knows?" I asked Splat. "He seems pretty upset."

"Nah. Probably just ran out of matches."

I went over and knocked on the door. "You okay in there?"

A muffled voice said, "Go away!"

"Reminds me of when my cousin Jimmy used to lock himself in his room," Splat said. "Let me handle this." He raised his voice. "Hey, Niles, we got cake and ice cream out here." When there was no answer, Splat shook his head. "Funny, it always worked with Jimmy."

The next office was empty. I went inside and dialed Denton's extension.

"Denton here," said the voice at the other end.

"Niles, it's me."

"Get off the line, Szyznowski. This is police property."

"Are you all right?" I asked.

127

"Yes, I'm fine."

"This doesn't have anything to do with the Lim case, does it?"

"As a matter of fact, it does," he said. "Now if you don't mind, I have work to do."

"You know, Niles, whenever you feel bad it always helps to talk about it."

"I'm going to hang up now."

"So," I said, "I guess you don't want the new information we brought you."

"I told you to stay away from this case, Szyznowski." There was a pause. "What new information?"

"I've always disliked talking on the phone."

He sighed. "You don't give up, do you? Okay, get in here."

By the time we opened the door, Denton had assumed a Bogart pose—feet on the desk, hands behind the head, fedora tipped back, with a cigarette dangling from one side of his mouth. The only problem was that in Denton's case, the requisite five o'clock shadow had barely reached noon.

"Okay, Szyznowski, let's hear it."

"Not until you tell us why you're upset."

"Hey, that's cheating."

"We prefer to think of it as blackmail," said Splat.

Denton crossed his arms and stuck out his jaw. "You go first."

We started for the door. "Sorry we couldn't do business, Niles," I said.

"Wait," said Denton. He made a big production of crushing out his cigarette stub. Then he lit another one, straightened his fedora, and brushed off the lapels of his trench coat. "What happened was, I went to see Cantini."

"You got a search warrant!" said Splat. "Just like I told you."

"It had nothing to do with your suggestion," Denton said.

"Did too."

"Did not."

"Did too."

"Kids, kids," I said. "So, Niles, what did you get?"

He glared at Splat. "You want to know what I got? I'll tell you what I got. A lecture on sticking my nose into other people's business, that's what."

"No Strad?" said Splat.

"Oldest thing in the room was the sweater he was wearing."

"Can you get a search warrant for his house?" Splat asked.

"You don't understand, Pauling. I've tipped him off."

"He's right, Splat," I said. "By now, Cantini's hidden the violin someplace where we'll never find it."

"Oh, I'll find it," said Denton. "It'll just take me longer now."

"So you're admitting we were right about Cantini?" asked Splat.

Denton flicked the ashes from his cigarette. "I suspected him all along."

Splat looked at me and rolled his eyes.

"Okay, Szyznowski, I've spilled my guts," Denton said. "Now it's your turn."

I took a deep breath and filled him in on what had happened. I had to admit, he took it pretty well for a guy who was apoplectic with rage.

129

"You went to meet him without calling me?" he said, turning an attractive Paul Masson red.

"He told us not to tell you. Besides, he said he just wanted to talk."

I pulled the note out of my pocket and laid it in front of Denton. Suddenly he sat up straight. "The note says seven o'clock. Is that when all this happened?"

"Yeah, why?"

"I got to Cantini's studio about seven twenty. He had just driven up. Claimed he'd been to a movie."

"Yeah, *Cannonball Run*," said Splat.

"What do we do now?" I asked Denton.

"*We* don't do anything. I keep working on the case, and you kiddies toddle on home. Time for the big boys to take over."

"When they get here, can we meet them?" asked Splat.

"You're very funny, Pauling. If you lay off this case, maybe you'll live long enough to tell a few more jokes."

He scribbled something on a piece of paper and handed it to me. "This is my private line. If anything happens, call me. And I mean anything."

When I got home, my dad was sitting at the kitchen table with cookbooks spread out all around him. I went over and stood behind him.

"What are you working on?" I asked.

"I'm planning tomorrow night's menu. Splat and his mom are going to have a meal they'll never forget. I'll start them off with a little duck pâté."

"I've always liked little ducks."

"Next I'll bring on a *salade de boeuf à la Parisienne*, followed by potato soup with leeks."

"If it leaks, won't it mess up the tablecloth?"

"And for the grand finale I'm unveiling my latest and greatest creation, Salmon Szyznowski."

"Wow, what's that?"

"Something new. You'll see."

"Chez Dad. My favorite restaurant." I gave him a peck on the cheek.

He stood up and began collecting his books. "Tomorrow's my day off, so that's when I'll do all my shopping and cooking."

I had no way of knowing it, but as my dad spent the next day preparing Salmon Szyznowski, he would be doing a lot more than just baking a fish. He'd be cooking the goose of the Merry Prankster.

15

· · · · · · ·

Splat arrived with his mother at seven o'clock sharp. Sporting a blue blazer and tie, he was dressed to kill, or at the very least to maim.

He looked around the apartment. "Hey, the place looks nice. Flowers, candles, the whole bit."

"That's a lovely statue of a basset hound," said Gwendolyn.

Just then my dad came out of the kitchen. He was looking good, too, wearing his only suit and a brand-new pair of maroon Nikes.

"Ladies and gentlemen," I said, "Chef Raymond Szyznowski. Chef Raymond, this is Lady Gwendolyn Pauling and her escort, the Archduke of Packard."

My dad gave them a self-conscious nod. "Hey, Splat. How's it going, Gwen?" He extended his hand, and Gwendolyn gave it a brief squeeze, blushing furiously.

I took her wrap, and they sat down on the couch. Dad put on some early Miles Davis, then disappeared into the kitchen. A few minutes later he was back with a loaf of French bread and a tan concoction fanned out in slices on a plate.

"Duck pâté," he said. "Dig."

He set the dish in front of Gwendolyn and handed her a knife. She hesitated for a moment, then spread the pâté on some bread and took a small bite. Her eyes opened wide.

"My goodness," she said.

He wrung his hands nervously. "My goodness good, or my goodness bad?"

"My goodness wonderful."

Splat tried some, nodding appreciatively. "It's amazing what you can do by grinding up a few ducks."

"Why am I suddenly not hungry?" I said.

After a few minutes we adjourned to the table, where Gwendolyn *ooh*ed and *ah*ed over the *salade de boeuf à la Parisienne*. By the time we got to the potato soup with leeks, she was in such raptures over the food that she seemed to have gotten over some of her initial shyness.

"I hope you don't mind my asking," she ventured, "but how did you learn to cook like this?"

My dad shrugged. "Self defense, mostly. We were used to eating pretty well when Sizzle's mom was living with us. But she left when Sizzle was eight."

"Oh, I'm sorry," said Gwendolyn.

"So were we," I said.

"We still had to eat," he went on, "so I took a few cooking classes at the Free University. That was in Berkeley, where we were living back then. I was unemployed and watched a lot of TV, and I happened to come across a cooking show."

"The rest," I said, "is culinary history."

"Why did you leave Berkeley?" asked Splat.

My dad smiled sadly. "There's a bookstore on Telegraph Avenue where Sizzle's mother and I used to spend a lot of time. It was on a corner that I passed every day, and whenever I walked by I'd start feeling bad. It sounds funny, but I think the reason we left Berkeley was so I wouldn't have to walk by that bookstore anymore."

He ran a spoon through his soup, stirring it absently. Watching the others' faces, I had a sudden feeling that if I didn't speak up, the evening was in danger of collapsing like a bad soufflé.

"Now you've heard all about us," I said. "What about you?"

"Tell them, Mom," said Splat.

"Oh, they're probably not interested."

"Do you like fairy tales?" Splat asked us.

"I've seen *Snow White* thirteen times," I said.

"This is the story," said Splat, "of a princess who lived in a magical kingdom called Boston."

"Oh, Arthur."

"I'd really like to hear about it," my dad said.

Gwendolyn smiled shyly, swirling her wine around in the glass. She took a deep breath, then emptied the glass and looked up at us. "You see, my family didn't have much money when I was young, so we didn't go to movies or things like that. Instead, my mother would tell me fairy tales. And no matter which tale it was, the heroine always had the same name."

"Gwendolyn," I said.

"That's right."

"Hansel and Gwendolyn," said Splat. "Has a nice ring to it, huh?"

I wondered how many times Splat had heard this story as he grew up, sitting by his mother's side in some small New England house. It occurred to me that even though the tale may have been told hundreds of times, we were probably the first outsiders to hear it. As Gwendolyn went on, her voice grew more confident.

"From the beginning my parents treated me like a princess. I was an only child, and they were both in their forties when I was born, so they were overprotective. The fact that I was small just made it worse. Mother didn't like me to go outside, so I'd stay in the house and play by myself. My only contact with the outside world came once a week, when my ballet teacher would give me lessons at home."

"Didn't you say your parents were poor?" my dad asked.

"Hey," said Splat, "when your daughter's a princess you're willing to make a few sacrifices."

"I met some other children when I started school, of course, but by that time I was completely absorbed in my own world. I'm afraid I never did learn how to make friends very well, and I looked so different from everyone else that they were hesitant to approach me."

"In the tenth grade she was still just three feet tall," Splat said.

"You say you're not good at making friends," I told her, "but you're doing okay with us."

"You're different," she said.

"Yeah," said Splat, "you're weird, like we are."

I started to say something but changed my mind. I had the oddest feeling I'd just gotten a compliment.

"When I was twenty years old," she said, "suddenly everything changed."

"She shot up to three feet ten," said Splat.

"And it was the year I met Arthur," Gwendolyn added.

I had a sudden vision of a zit-faced baby toddling up to Gwendolyn and introducing himself. "You 'met' your son?" I said. "Isn't that a funny way of putting it?"

She smiled. "Not my son. My husband, Arthur Hadley Reavis Pauling, Jr."

"What a guy," said Splat.

"He was from one of the oldest and proudest families in Boston. His father owned a Rolls Royce dealership, among other things, and his mother was president of the symphony association. Arthur was their only child, and . . . well, he was a little bit unusual."

"The word is *flake*," Splat said.

"It was hard for him, dear, growing up in a family like that. There was a great deal of pressure."

"Yeah," said Splat, "it was rough, not knowing where your next trust fund was coming from."

"Arthur's father had his whole life planned out for him—Exeter, Harvard, then back home to join the family business. He made it as far as Harvard."

"Was there a problem?" asked my dad.

"It was in the late sixties. People all around him were doing their own thing, and I guess he felt he was doing somebody else's. So he decided to leave school and do some traveling. His parents didn't hear from him for three years, and then suddenly one day, there he was on their doorstep."

"Probably tired of eating canned soup," said Splat.

"He asked if he could work at the car dealership, and of course his father was delighted. A few weeks later he went to a piano recital and saw me in the audience. It was love at first sight, just like in the fairy tales."

"They got married a couple months later," Splat said.

Gwendolyn reached over and opened her purse. She pulled out a photograph and passed it to me. "There he is—my Prince Charming."

I can now verify that love is blind. Prince Charming looked just like Splat, bad complexion and all.

"My God, there are two of them," I murmured.

"Pardon me?" said Gwendolyn.

"Uh, two eyes, two ears, two nostrils—it's amazing when you think about it."

"At first there were some raised eyebrows in Arthur's family about my size and social status, but they got over it. They came to realize that in a funny way I was as refined as they were because of the way my parents had brought me up. Anyway, Arthur and I were happy, and that was all that really mattered."

"Come on, get to the good part," said Splat.

"Which part is that, dear?" she asked.

"Me," he said.

"Ah, yes. Little Arthur was born a year later."

"What happened to your husband?" I asked Gwendolyn.

A look of embarrassment crossed her face. "He left two years after the baby was born. But I don't blame him, I really don't."

"I do," said Splat.

"He was never meant for that kind of life. He tried hard, but it just didn't suit him."

Splat shrugged. "He ran away. Great guy, huh?"

"He liked bowling and I liked ballet. He wanted to wear jeans, and I enjoyed dressing up in a pretty evening gown. I'm afraid it just wasn't meant to be."

It was ironic, I thought. Splat's father was well bred on the outside and humble inside; his mother was just the reverse. Each of them wanted to be what the other was, and somewhere in between they had passed each other, like yachts in the night.

"They got divorced when I was three," said Splat. "Every month she gets a fat check for alimony and child support."

"Do you ever see your dad anymore?" I asked.

"Nah," said Splat. "He's probably managing a pool hall someplace, happy as a clam. Wherever he is, though, he's not making much money, because our checks come from his parents."

"He's doing what he has to, dear, I'm sure," said Gwendolyn.

"How did you end up out here?" my dad asked.

"I'd gone back to live with my parents after the divorce," she said. "They helped me raise Arthur. Then a year ago, when Arthur was sixteen, both my parents died, and I decided we should move to Los Angeles."

"Why?" I asked.

"L.A.'s the ultimate fairy tale," said Splat. "Can you

think of a better place for a princess to live happily ever after?"

"Besides," she said, "now we know it has the finest French restaurant in the country. And I don't mean Chez Pierre."

"Speaking of which," I said, "I'm hungry again. Is there any more food?"

"Coming right up," said the chef. I helped him clear the dishes away, and a few minutes later he emerged from the kitchen carrying a large covered platter. He set it down in the middle of the table.

"Ladies and gentlemen," he said, "we're proud to present our featured entree for the evening, Salmon Szyznowski. Ta-da!" He removed the cover with a flourish.

"Wow," Splat said.

"Good heavens," Gwendolyn said.

"Holy jumping tamales," I said.

It didn't look like any food I'd ever seen. It didn't even look like any picture of food I'd ever seen.

What it looked like was a work of art.

The salmon was positioned in the middle, topped with hollandaise sauce and slivers of avocado. Lemon slices lined the edges like small half-moons, surrounded by chopped parsley and dill. But the real pièce de résistance was the salmon, cooked plump and pink by the grinning chef.

"That's some fish you got there," I said.

"This doesn't belong on a plate," said Splat. "It belongs on a wall at the Metropolitan Museum. Of course, then it might slide off."

"Let's just be glad it's here for us to eat," his mother said.

"Do we have to cut into it?" Splat asked.

"Hey, some of us here are hungry," I said. "Not to be crude or anything."

"You're right, Sizzle," my dad said, picking up a serving fork and knife. "It's nice if food looks good, but the important thing is how it tastes."

He put a slice of salmon on each of our plates, spooning some of the assorted goodies over it. Then he sat back and watched. Silence descended on the room as the three of us tried our first bite.

How do you describe a flavor? What word could possibly capture the feeling you get when tasting a new dish for the first time?

In this case, the word was *Goodyear*. Salmon Szyznowski tasted like old tires.

"Well?" said my dad.

"Interesting," Gwendolyn murmured.

Splat nodded. "Never tasted anything quite like it."

"Dad, do you love me?" I asked.

"Huh? Sure."

"How much?"

"What's wrong?" he asked.

"The salmon," I replied.

He tried a bite, then looked up at me, his face pale with shock. He bore the look of a man who returns home one day to find that his house is gone. "I . . . it . . . we . . ."

I reached over and patted his arm. "It's okay, Dad. It looked beautiful."

He stared at the fish, his lips moving soundlessly.

"Come on, Mr. Szyznowski," said Splat, "even Babe Ruth had a few bad days at the plate."

140

"Great time for a pun," I snapped.

"What did I say?"

My dad sighed, regaining the use of his larynx. "I knew I shouldn't have done it."

"What's that?" asked Gwendolyn.

"I broke the cardinal rule of entertaining: Never try out a new dish on guests. The first time you cook something, it probably won't be very good."

Somewhere in the back of my mind, there was a click as the last piece of a puzzle fell into place.

I knew the secret of the Merry Prankster.

I excused myself and made three quick phone calls. The last one was to Niles Denton.

"That's ridiculous," said Denton. "You can't base an entire case on a little detail like that."

"It's not little. It's the key to the whole thing."

"I'm telling you, Szyznowski, forget it. You're coming out of left field."

"Okay, don't say I didn't give you a shot at it."

"I don't like the sound of that," he said. "What are you going to do?"

"Take a little stroll in the ballpark. I've heard left field can be pretty interesting."

16

. . . .

"How do you know he'll be there?" Splat asked me.

"He told us himself. He spends every evening playing his violin."

It was later that night, and we were in the Packard, on our way to Pasadena.

"I don't know about this, Sizzle," he said.

"I'm not too crazy about it myself. But since Denton won't follow through, we'll just have to do it ourselves."

"I'm not referring to that. I'm talking about leaving my mom alone with your dad."

"Yeah, he's a pretty vicious guy," I said.

"My mom's very fragile."

"Not as fragile as you think."

"Sizzle, she hasn't been alone with anyone but me for the last year."

"After that, she should be ready for anything." I pointed to a sign. "Here's our exit. Get off and hang a right."

He followed my directions, turning south toward Colorado Boulevard. "You could at least tell me what we're going to do."

"Listen," I said.

"I am listening."

"No, I mean that's what we're going to do."

"I don't get it."

"You will."

A few minutes later we were on the block where Giuseppe Cantini's studio was located. Splat started to pull up in front.

"Don't stop," I said.

"I thought we were going to see Cantini."

"Not exactly."

I had him turn at the next corner. He parked halfway down the street and switched off the engine.

"Now what do we do?" he asked.

"Wait."

"Good. That'll give you a chance to explain what's going on."

"Splat," I said, "we've been overlooking one entire category of evidence. It's the most important part of the whole case."

"That's impossible."

"Not at all. The reason we overlooked it is that it's invisible."

He gave me a funny look. "What are we talking about here? Flying saucers? Little green men?"

"I'm talking about sound—the sound a Stradivarius makes, as opposed to a reproduction."

"What makes you think we can tell the difference?"

"We can't," I said, "but we know someone who can. And if I'm not mistaken, here he comes now."

A Honda Civic pulled up behind us. "Hey, isn't that Kevin Lim's car?" said Splat. "I thought he was grounded."

"He is. I called him before we left."

Kevin got out and walked up to the open window of the Packard. "I told my folks I was going to the library to study. If I'm not back in an hour or so they'll start getting suspicious."

"We'll try to make it quick," I said. "Come on, Splat."

We headed up the street, and on the way I briefly told Kevin our theory about Buffy Dupree switching instruments and giving the Strad to Cantini.

"You mean my father's violin might not have been destroyed?" asked Kevin.

I nodded. "We think Cantini has it. We'd like you to listen to him play and tell us if we're right."

"What makes you think he'll be playing it tonight?"

"He told us he plays every night," Splat said.

"He also said that fine instruments cry out to be played," I said. "Well, if he's got the Strad it should be shrieking right about now. I'm betting he won't be able to resist."

We slipped into the alley next to Cantini's building. There was a late-model car parked outside the studio, and we hid behind it in case anyone should come along. Through a high window we could see that the studio light was on.

"I don't hear any shrieks," whispered Splat.

"Just be patient, wise guy."

Ten minutes later there was still no sound, and I was starting to get worried. Maybe he didn't play every night after all. Maybe he just forgot to turn off the light and was out somewhere downing a plate of linguine and clam sauce.

Kevin looked nervously at his watch. "I don't know how much longer I'll be able to stay."

As if on cue, the music started. It was a Paganini sonata, played as Paganini himself might have played it. The tone was rich and lustrous. The intonation was impeccable. Every note was perfectly shaped and molded, like features on a marble statue.

"Hey," Splat said, "that guy's good."

"Is he?" I asked. "Or is it the violin?"

"You're right, it must be the Strad!" said Splat.

We looked over at Kevin. He was listening intently, his head cocked to the side and his eyes half-closed. Finally he shook his head apologetically. "I'd like to help you, but there's no way of telling for sure."

"But it's possible that could be the Strad?" I asked.

"Yeah, it's possible. It sounds good enough, that's for sure."

I turned to Splat. "We've got our man. Let's get out of here."

I turned and headed down the alley. Splat and Kevin exchanged puzzled glances, then followed along behind.

"Excuse me, but did I miss something?" said Splat when we got back to the car.

"Yeah," I said. "And so did I for a long time."

"So your theory was right about Cantini and Buffy Dupree?" asked Kevin.

"As a matter of fact, no. We just disproved it."

"Excuse me," said Splat, "but I'm lost."

"It's pretty simple," I told him. "You can sum it up in one little riddle: What does a Stradivarius have in common with Salmon Szyznowski?"

"They both start with *S*?" said Splat.

"Try again."

"They look better than they taste?"

"Not exactly. What they have in common is that neither one works very well the first time you try it."

"Hey, that's right," said Splat. "Cantini told us it takes weeks to learn how to play a Stradivarius really well."

"So," I said, "chances are it wasn't the Strad we just heard him playing. Right, Kevin?"

Kevin nodded. "Yeah, I forgot all about that."

"I'm surprised you'd forget," I said, "since the same thing must have happened to you. Don't you remember the first time you played your father's Stradivarius? It was at the rehearsal the day of the fireworks, if I'm not mistaken. You played the Tchaikovsky concerto."

"Wait a second," said Splat. "Kevin sounded great that day."

"Well, that wasn't exactly the first time I'd played it," he said. "I'd tried it a few times already, so I'd gotten pretty good on it."

"That's not what you told us before," Splat said.

"You know, Kevin," I said, "I think I've heard you play your father's violin. But it wasn't at that rehearsal. It was at your house three days later, when I came by to see you."

Kevin was looking down at his sleeve, where he'd developed a sudden interest in a piece of lint.

"Remember?" I said. "You sounded awful. At the time, you gave me some excuse about practicing things you weren't good at. But that wasn't it, was it? The real reason was the instrument. It was your father's Strad, and you weren't used to it yet. With your parents gone, it was a chance for you to play it."

"Back up a second," said Splat. "If it wasn't the Strad he was playing at the rehearsal, what was it?"

"A reproduction. I called Cantini before we came over tonight, and he told me he'd sold one just a few days before that rehearsal. The buyer was Kevin Lim."

"So our theory was right," Splat said. "We just had the wrong person."

When Kevin finally looked up at us, he spoke with a depth of feeling I hadn't heard before. "My father didn't deserve to have that violin. He didn't love it the way I did. When he first bought it ten years ago, I'd spend hours listening to him play. When he'd set it down and go to another room, I'd get right up next to it and study every inch, imagining what it would feel like to run my hand along the wood."

"You didn't touch it?" asked Splat.

Kevin shook his head. "He wouldn't let me. But I knew the sound of it like I knew my own voice, and I always dreamed about playing it someday. That's what got me started on the violin in the first place. I just wanted to be good enough to play that Stradivarius. But I never did. Not in all those years."

"Come on, Kevin," I said. "You must have sneaked in and played it sometime."

"Yeah," said Splat, "or at least copped a quick feel."

"You don't know my father," said Kevin. "He's got a terrible temper. If you break his rules, you pay." He stared off into space, and for a moment I could almost see the stern face of Bradford Lim glaring back.

"Finally," he said, "something snapped. I don't know what did it, but suddenly I couldn't stand it anymore. I wanted to have that violin for my own."

"So you dreamed up the Merry Prankster," I said.

He nodded. "I was getting the Tchaikovsky music from Arnie Klingmeyer, and I noticed we'd also be playing *Till Eulenspiegel's Merry Pranks*. That's when I got the idea. I had Arnie show me all the pieces we'd be playing during spring break, then I went home and planned everything.

"I'm pretty good with electrical wiring, and my uncle owns a fish store, so the first two pranks were easy. I knew everyone would suspect Myron. I even stole those pigeons from his neighbor to make sure Myron got the blame."

"How did you know about them?" asked Splat.

"I scouted out Myron's house when I was planning the pranks and met that guy Benny. When I saw his pigeons, I got the idea for the winged messenger."

"But Kevin," I said, "you weren't even at the rehearsal the day of that prank. You'd been grounded by then, hadn't you?"

"Yeah, but I was able to sneak out the night before. I got the pigeons and took them into the rehearsal hall through a side door I'd propped open earlier that day. Mr. Pirelli never locks his office, so it was no problem putting the pigeons in there."

"We know that for the *Royal Fireworks* prank you went to Cantini and bought one of his reproductions," I said. "But how did you light the firecrackers without anyone noticing?"

"It was easy. I did it with the case half-closed, then left it on the chair and walked across the room. By the time the first firecracker went off, I was in the middle of a conversation with Mr. Pirelli."

"When you tried to put the fire out," said Splat, "did you burn your hands on purpose?"

"Yes. But I was careful not to burn them too badly."

"Kevin, I guess I can understand hurting yourself to get something you want," I said. "But it's not fair to put other people in danger."

He chuckled. "I'd hardly call dead fish dangerous. And a little water never hurt anybody."

"How about a little cannon?" Splat said.

"What do you mean?"

"You know," said Splat, "Pachelbel's weapon of choice."

"We weren't too crazy about Bach's or Rossini's, either," I said.

Kevin stared blankly at us. "I don't understand."

"The other pranks, Kevin," I said.

"The last prank I played was with the pigeons," Kevin said, his face pale. "I even said so in the note."

"Either he's telling the truth," I said to Splat, "or he's a better actor than he is a violinist."

"Tell me what happened," Kevin said.

I briefly described the other incidents. When I was done, he looked at us almost pleadingly. "You don't really believe I'd try those things, do you?"

"Somebody did," said Splat.

"I'm grounded, remember?" Kevin said. "I sneaked out once, but there's no way I could have pulled all those other pranks."

"There's an alibi you'll never hear on 'Perry Mason,' " said Splat. " 'Your honor, the defendant couldn't possibly have committed this murder, because he was grounded.' "

Kevin shivered. "Don't even say that word."

"*Perry?*"

"*Murder*. Whoever did this, I can't believe they were trying to kill you."

"Fifty million bees can't be wrong," Splat said.

Kevin looked at his watch. "I've been gone over an hour. I've got to get home."

He took a few steps toward his car, then turned back.

"You're not going to do anything, are you?"

"Yeah," I said. "We're just not sure what."

17

• • • • • • •

"I think he's telling the truth," I said as we arrived back home.

"I think you're getting soft in the head," said Splat. "The guy admits he did it, then says he's only half guilty. Give me a break."

"I don't know, Splat. Can you imagine Kevin Lim trying to hurt somebody?"

"We're talking about a guy who purposely stuck his hands in a fire. At this point nothing would surprise me. Besides, if Kevin didn't do it, who did?"

Splat's unanswered question hung in the air as we climbed the stairs to my apartment and went inside. It was a warm evening, so I left the door open, shutting only the screen. When I looked around the place, the dishes were still on the table, but otherwise there was no sign of life. Of course, Mellow was lying in the corner, but that didn't count.

"Dad?" I called, checking the other rooms. "Gwendolyn?" There was no answer.

When I came back into the living room, Splat had picked up a note from the coffee table. He read it to me. " 'Gone for a walk. Back in a while. Love, Dad.' "

Splat looked up at me, his face tense. "My God, where would they go?"

"I don't know. Häagen-Dazs, maybe. There's one about a mile down the road."

"My mom hasn't been on a walk in fifteen years."

"They're not trekking across the Sahara. This is Mar Vista. There are sidewalks and everything."

"What if something happens? I'd never forgive myself."

"Splat, your mom may be short, but she's a grown woman. Anyway, she's with my dad."

"Great. The man who brought you Salmon Szyznowski."

I shot him a Charles Bronson glare.

"Sorry," he said. "I just worry, that's all."

"Don't. We've got more important things to do."

"Such as?"

"Think. And for that, I need music."

I pulled out a few records and put on Tchaikovsky's Sixth Symphony. Then I sat down on the couch, propped up my feet on the coffee table, and listened as the low, mournful theme began in the bassoons and basses.

"The question is," I said, "who besides Kevin would want to scare us off the case?"

Splat plopped down next to me. He tore off a piece of French bread and used it to scoop up some duck pâté. Then he gazed across the room, chewing thoughtfully.

"Cantini? He's the one who sold Kevin the reproduction. Maybe they're in this together."

I shook my head. "Doesn't make sense. Kevin would have told us if he had a partner."

"Maybe Kevin didn't know about it. Cantini could have figured it out on his own."

"Yeah, I guess," I said. "But why would he try to stop us from finding out? Why would he even care?"

Splat shrugged. "I never said my theory was perfect."

"To me," I said, "the amazing thing is that the second prankster knew about Kevin before we did."

"But how could they have found out?"

"Well, we found out by hearing him practice. Maybe somebody else did, too."

"I suppose it would have to be a person familiar with Strads," said Splat.

We both looked at each other and uttered the same name at the same time: "Bradford Lim."

From across the room came a voice as cold and brittle as a sheet of ice. "I'm afraid you are far too clever."

The screen door opened, and Bradford Lim stepped inside. He was wearing an overcoat, and his right hand was in a pocket.

Splat gaped. "Where did you come from?"

"Pasadena. I was listening to an interesting conversation between my son and two nosy friends."

"You followed Kevin?" I asked.

153

"Yes. You see, the library is closed on Mondays."

"Woops," said Splat.

"My son isn't very good with details. It's one of many reasons he'll never be a great violinist."

"So you overheard what he told us," I said.

"I most certainly did. Then I followed you here, and when I heard the music I came upstairs, where you'd been thoughtful enough to leave the door open."

"We're like that," said Splat. "Very considerate."

"It's true, then," I said. "You did hear Kevin playing the Strad."

"That's right. I came home early from rehearsal one day, and he didn't hear me drive up. His playing sounded even worse than usual. I knew it had to be my violin."

"Why didn't you just barge inside and tear his head off, the way any normal father would?" asked Splat.

"That, of course, is precisely what I wanted to do. But by this time there was more involved than punishing a disobedient child. For one thing, I couldn't simply take the violin back and begin playing it again. Things had become more complicated."

"Are you talking about the police?" I asked.

"No, Miss Szyznowski, I'm speaking of something far more complex and Byzantine than police procedures will ever be."

"The *New York Times* crossword puzzle?" said Splat.

"I'm referring to insurance," Lim said. "I was settling a claim for two hundred and fifty thousand dollars."

"But you had the violin back," I said. "If you wanted money, why not just sell it?"

154

"I didn't care about the money. It was only the means to something else, something even better than owning a Stradivarius."

"And what was that?" I asked.

"Owning two Stradivariuses."

"I think that's Stradivarii," said Splat.

"I'd located another one through a colleague in Sweden and had already made arrangements to buy it. Beautiful instrument. Fully as good as my first."

"Not bad," Splat said. "This way you could have your violin and eat it, too."

"Why haven't you told Kevin that you know what he did?" I asked. "He'd have to find out sometime, or you'd never be able to play your first Stradivarius."

"Oh, I would have told him eventually. But I was conducting some delicate negotiations with the insurance company and didn't want anything to go wrong."

"Such as Kevin's nosy friends finding out that the instrument was never destroyed?" I said.

Lim nodded. "That's why I became the Merry Prankster, as I'm sure you've guessed by now."

"How did you know about the Prankster and the rhymed notes and everything?" asked Splat.

"The police kept me informed about the investigation. They showed me the note and gave me all the information I needed in order to take over my son's role as the Merry Prankster."

"So then you followed us all around, playing those tricks, right?" I said.

"Correct. I was especially proud of the music box, which was meant to make you suspect my old rival, Cantini."

"It would have worked if it weren't for Salmon Szyz-nowski," I said.

"I beg your pardon?"

"Let's just say we thought something was fishy," said Splat.

"Now that we know your secret," I asked Lim, "what are you going to do?"

"That's simple," he replied. "I have to kill you."

Bradford Lim drew his hand out of the overcoat pocket. He was holding a gun.

"Mr. Lim," said Splat, "I don't want to question your judgment or anything, but are you nuts?"

"I assure you, Mr. Pauling, I know exactly what I'm doing."

"If you fire that gun," I said, "the neighbors will hear you."

"I don't think so." He reached into his coat pocket and pulled out a cassette. Then he stepped over to the stereo, holding the gun on us all the while, and loaded the tape into the machine. The Sixth Symphony stopped, and the measured tones of a string choir began.

"The *1812* Overture," I said. "Nice piece—especially the part with the cannons."

Lim smiled and turned up the volume. "I don't think the neighbors will notice a few pistol shots, do you?"

If I remembered correctly, the cannons came in toward the end of the overture. That gave us a little over five minutes to think of something.

"You're a very thorough man," I said. "Unfortunately you overlooked one small detail—my dog, Rambo."

"Rambo?" murmured Splat.

"He's trained to kill on command," I told Lim. Suddenly I shouted, "Rambo, attack!"

Mellow may have twitched his left eyebrow; I'm not sure.

I shrugged. "It was worth a try."

"You know," said Splat, "our parents will be back in a minute. They went for a walk."

"Sorry, Mr. Pauling, it's not going to work."

"Really, I'll show you the note." Splat took a step toward the coffee table.

"Don't move!" said Lim, waving the pistol menacingly.

"It wasn't very well written, anyway," Splat said.

"Mr. Lim, think about what you're doing," I said. "Is it really worth killing two people over a musical instrument, even if it is a Stradivarius?"

"Probably not. But there's more at stake than that. I've committed insurance fraud, and my 'pranks' to scare you off could be seen as murder attempts. If any of this comes out, my career will be ruined. Fortunately, you are the only two people in the world who know about it. Other than my son, of course."

"Speaking of your son," I said, "would you believe me if I said he was standing outside the door right now?"

"Hi, Kevin," said Splat. "We were just talking about you."

Lim chuckled. "I can see how you solved this mystery. You're persistent, and you have quite an imagination."

"Personally I think they're just lucky," said Kevin. He opened the screen door and walked in, holding a violin case.

Startled, Lim whirled around. As he did, Splat lunged at him. Lim saw Splat out of the corner of his eye and staggered backward at the last minute, shoving Splat away with his free hand. He retreated to the stereo, still holding the gun on us, his hand shaking visibly. He glanced at Kevin.

"What are you doing here?" he said.

"I figured out who the other prankster had to be," said Kevin. "I came here to warn them, but I don't think I really believed it until just now."

"Kevin, I want you to go home," said Lim. "I'll explain everything when I get back."

"Explain it now," Kevin said. "Why are you pointing a gun at my friends?"

"Do as I say," Lim hissed.

Kevin blinked a couple of times but stood his ground. "I always thought you were strong. But you're not. You have to sneak around and lie to get what you want."

His father smiled grimly. "I seem to have taught you well."

"I admired you," said Kevin. "I wanted to be just like you and play the violin. But you had to be the center of attention. You didn't want any competition, even from your own son."

The tempo of the music picked up, and so did my heartbeat. The French army was starting to roll its cannons into place. I figured we had a minute, maybe two, before they lit the fuse.

"I'm sorry, Kevin," said Lim, leveling his gun at Splat and me, "but I'm afraid I have some business to take care of. Perhaps we can discuss your unhappy childhood some other time."

"I don't know about you guys," said Splat, "but he's got my nomination as Father of the Year."

"Shut up, Splat," said Kevin. He turned to his father. "Please, don't do this."

"I have to," Lim said.

"It's not too late," Kevin pleaded. "We could go to the police. I'd help you."

Lim gazed at his son, and I could have sworn I saw a crack in his icy facade.

"Dad, I love you," said Kevin.

"Why?" asked Lim, a look of something like pain on his face.

"If you love me even a little bit, put down the gun."

There was a distant fanfare in the horns as Napoleon's army prepared to fire. Lim straightened his shoulders and did the same.

"I'm sorry, Kevin," he said.

Kevin shook his head sadly, then knelt down and opened the violin case he'd brought in. For one crazy minute I had visions of him pulling out a machine gun. Then I saw that it was a violin. I didn't need to see the look in his father's eyes to know it was the Strad.

Kevin stood up. "If you don't stop, I'm going to destroy this instrument."

"Put it away," Lim said, licking his lips nervously.

His son opened the screen door and went outside. "I'm going to drop it off the balcony," he said. "It'll break on the sidewalk."

Droplets of perspiration stood out on Lim's forehead. "You won't do it. That instrument means too much to you."

"I love you more," Kevin answered.

159

As he held the Strad over the railing, the trumpets flared, the cymbals crashed, and the cannons began to roar. Lim's glance flicked from his son to us and back again. His whole arm was quivering so badly that for a second I thought the vibration alone might set off the trigger. Out on the balcony, Kevin yelled something, but the cannons and the fireworks and the church bells drowned him out.

Then Kevin opened his hand and dropped the violin.

With a cry of pain, Bradford Lim threw down his weapon and charged through the screen door to the balcony.

"Get the gun," Splat said quickly.

I grabbed it. When I looked up, Lim was standing at the rail, staring downward.

"Come on out," his son told us. "It's okay now."

We cautiously made our way out onto the balcony, and Kevin pointed to the ground below. When Splat glanced down, his eyes opened wide.

"I don't know if I even want to look," I said.

"Sure you do," said a voice from below.

As the French army marched to victory, I peeked over the railing.

"Yo, Szyznowski," said Detective Niles Denton. He was holding the Stradivarius, and there wasn't a scratch on it.

18

•••••••

We stood with Kevin in front of my apartment, watching from a distance as Niles Denton and two other police officers talked to Bradford Lim. Lim spoke with his head down, clutching the violin case to his chest and staring at the sidewalk. Denton was nodding and taking notes in a small notebook he'd pulled from the pocket of his trench coat. Behind them, the patrol car's flashing lights cast an eerie red glow on the side of the building, and the police radio spit out messages over the buzz of the assembled crowd.

"How did you know your father did it?" Splat asked Kevin.

"Maybe he doesn't want to talk about it," I said.

"It's okay," said Kevin. He gave a little shake of his head and scuffed at the dirt with his toe. "When I got home from Pasadena, I decided to tell my father what I'd done. I didn't want him finding out from anybody but me. I asked my mom where he was, and she told me he was gone. She said the minute I'd left for the library my father ran into the den, then drove off in a big hurry."

"What was in the den?" said Splat.

"Lots of things. But the only thing missing was his gun."

"Is that when you knew?" I asked.

Kevin nodded. "All the way home I'd been trying to figure out who the other prankster was, and when I saw that the gun was missing, things suddenly became very clear. My father must have found out what I'd done, then pulled more pranks to try to scare you off. I thought about the bees and the arrow and the cannon, and then I thought about the gun. That's when I decided to come warn you. I brought the violin, figuring it might come in handy."

"It sure did," I said. "You know, that's where you were wrong about your father. He really loves that Strad. You could tell by the way he acted when you dropped it."

"Too bad he doesn't feel the same way about his family," said Splat.

"He's not the only one guilty of that," Kevin said.

"What do you mean?" I asked.

"It's a funny thing. After my big speech about how I loved him more than the violin, I looked out over the railing and suddenly knew I couldn't destroy that instrument. I wouldn't have dropped it if Detective Denton

162

hadn't come along. Maybe I'm more like my father than I thought."

"Or he's more like you," I said.

"Maybe," said Kevin, gazing over toward his dad.

Across the way, Denton put away his notebook, and the police officers led Bradford Lim away.

"I've got to go," Kevin said. "My father's going to be needing my help, and I want to be around when he realizes that."

"Take care," said Splat.

"I will. You know, it may sound strange, but I'm glad you guys found out who the Merry Prankster was."

I squeezed his shoulder. "Me, too. Good luck, Kevin."

He gave me a shaky grin, then headed off to join his dad. A few minutes later, the police drove them away and the crowd dispersed. We walked over to Denton.

"So our idea was out of left field, huh?" I said.

Denton sighed. "Now I suppose I'll have to listen to a blow-by-blow account of how you solved the big case."

"That's right," said Splat. "And if you pay attention, you might even learn a thing or two."

We described the evening's events, from the meeting in Pasadena to the scene on the apartment balcony. Denton listened, his arms crossed.

"You're lucky you weren't killed," he said. "You know that, don't you?"

Splat shrugged. "All in a day's work."

"How do you figure it?" said Denton. "Lim has it all—talent, fame, money—and he throws it away for a few sticks somebody glued together three hundred years ago. A dame, I could understand. But this?"

" 'A fine violin is like a woman,' " I murmured.

"What's that again?" said Denton.

"Nothing. Just thinking out loud."

"What I don't understand," Splat said to Denton, "is what you were doing here tonight."

"After Szyznowski called," he replied, "I came over to make sure you wouldn't do anything stupid. No one was home, so I went up to the corner for a cup of coffee. When I came back, the Lim kid was out on the balcony, about to deep-six the fiddle. I figured if he didn't want it, I could use it for my trophy case."

"Talk about lucky timing," Splat said.

Denton shook his head. "Sheer instinct. All the great ones have it."

He dropped his cigarette butt and crushed it out with the toe of his shoe. "Well, kiddos, it's been real. Try to stay out of trouble, huh? At least for a few hours."

"You're okay, Niles," I said. "Not great, but okay."

"You're not bad yourself, Szyznowski."

"What about me?" asked Splat.

"You," he said, looking Splat up and down, "are something else."

Denton straightened his fedora, pulled the trench coat collar up around his neck, and moved off into the night.

We watched him go, then headed back to the apartment. "Well," said Splat, "another case bites the dust."

"A couple of brass players almost did, too."

"Yeah, but think of all the fun we had."

"You're right," I said. "There's nothing quite as exhilarating as staring down the barrel of a gun."

"And just think—we did it together."

"Is my heart supposed to do a little flip-flop, or what?"

Before he could answer, I noticed two figures approaching us on the sidewalk.

"Hello, there," called my dad.

Splat rushed up to his mother. "Where have you been?"

She stood on tiptoes and gave him a peck on the cheek. "Raymond and I went for a long walk into town. Lovely night, isn't it?"

"I guess," said Splat. "Weren't you nervous?"

"Maybe a little at first. But after a while I was fine."

"I convinced her she needed some excitement in her life," my dad said. "I knew we weren't going to get it staying at the apartment."

"That's for sure," I said, glancing at Splat. "Nothing ever happens around here."

"You know," said Gwendolyn, "thanks to Raymond, I realized something tonight."

"What's that, Mom?" said Splat.

"The world isn't such a dangerous place after all."

"What about you guys?" asked my dad. "What did you do after dinner?"

"Uh, this and that," said Splat quickly, looking at me for help.

"Mostly that," I said. "We'll tell you about it later."

"Come on in for dessert," my dad said. "Chocolate mousse."

"You two go ahead," I said. "We'll be with you in a minute."

They walked up the stairs, my dad's hand resting lightly on Gwendolyn's shoulder. When they were inside, I turned to Splat.

"Okay, what are we going to do?"

"Eat the mousse, I guess. Unless you'd rather go get some fries and a malt."

"You know very well what I mean."

"We'll tell them everything tomorrow," said Splat. "I just didn't want to ruin her evening."

"I'm not worried about that. I'm worried about *them.*"

"Huh?"

"How could you miss it?" I said. "They were acting like a pair of lovebirds."

"Sizzle, are you nuts? They weren't even touching."

"They were touching, I'm sure of it. It was a definite touch."

"Okay, so his hand might have brushed her arm."

"Do you realize what this means?"

"Wow, you're right," he said. "Cooties!"

"They might start dating."

"Don't be ridiculous. They're parents."

"If they start dating, they might fall in love. And if they fall in love, they might get engaged. And if they get engaged . . ."

"Nah, it's impossible," he said.

"You think so?"

"She's too short. He's too tall. I think it's illegal."

He paused a moment and looked off into space. "On the other hand, it does raise an interesting possibility."

"What's that?"

"Think about it."

I thought about it. "Holy cow."

"Wouldn't it be great?" said Splat.

"Pardon me, but I'm feeling slightly nauseous."

"Arthur Hadley Reavis Pauling Szyznowski. What a concept."

"Oh, brother."

"Exactly."

I groaned.

He grinned.

The Merry Prankster would have loved it.

ABOUT THE AUTHOR

Author RONALD KIDD says: "Somewhere along the line, people got the idea that orchestra musicians are just a bunch of humorless prigs. And it's true. Well, actually, only a few are, and those few provide the rest of the orchestra with a perfect target for practical jokes. I wondered what would happen if the jokes got out of hand, and *Second Fiddle* is the result."

Mr. Kidd is the author of *Sizzle* & *Splat*, *The Glitch*, *Dunker*, *That's What Friends Are For*, *Who Is Felix the Great?* and other books. In addition, he produces children's records for the Walt Disney Company. He and his wife live in Pasadena, California.